SOLAR BOUND

BOUND TRILOGY INSTALLMENT

GALAXY ALIEN MAIL ORDER BRIDES
BOOK EIGHT

MICHELLE M. PILLOW

MICHELLEPILLOW.COM

Sci-fi Paranormal Romantic Comedy

He glows. She burns. Together, they're impossible to hide.

When Solar, a golden-skinned guard from the eternal daylight of Solarus, crash-lands outside Duskrock, Arizona, subtlety goes up in smoke. The catastrophically inept Galaxy Alien Mail Order Brides have blown his cover, UFO headlines are everywhere, and a black-ops outfit called Milano is already on the hunt. Then Solar meets Dani Ember, a fire dancer whose spark pulls him like gravity, and hiding becomes the last thing on his mind.

Dani has always trusted flame more than people until an alien warrior explodes into her life, glowing like sunlight made flesh. Forced into hiding together, their connection ignites hotter with every touch. But with aliens Eclipse and Lunar also in Milano's crosshairs, duty and desire collide. To save his companions, protect Earth, and give his divided world a chance at peace, Solar must make the one choice he never planned for... claiming the human who feels like home.

--

SOLAR BOUND is a steamy sci-fi paranormal romantic comedy with a grumpy golden alien and a sunshine fire dancer, forced proximity on Earth, sizzling open-door heat, black-ops hunters, and a guaranteed HEA with no cliffhanger.

Book two of the Bound Trilogy installment from the Galaxy Alien Mail Order Brides series.

Dragon Lords Series

Barbarian Prince

Perfect Prince

Dark Prince

Warrior Prince

His Highness The Duke

The Stubborn Lord

The Reluctant Lord

The Impatient Lord

The Dragon's Queen

Lords of the Var Series

The Savage King

The Playful Prince
The Bound Prince
The Rogue Prince
The Pirate Prince

Captured by a Dragon-Shifter Series
Determined Prince
Rebellious Prince
Stranded with the Cajun
Hunted by the Dragon
Mischievous Prince
Headstrong Prince

Space Lords Series
His Frost Maiden
His Fire Maiden
His Metal Maiden
His Earth Maiden
His Woodland Maiden

Dynasty Lords Series

Seduction of the Phoenix

Temptation of the Butterfly

To learn more about the Qurilixen World series of books and to stay up to date on the latest book list visit www.MichellePillow.com

AUTHOR UPDATES

To stay informed about when a new book in the series installments is released, sign up for updates:

michellepillow.com/author-updates

WELCOME TO GALAXY BRIDES

A NOTE FROM THE AUTHOR

Dear Readers,

For those of you familiar with my bestselling series, Dragon Lords, you've already been introduced to the Galaxy Brides Corporation and the services they offer lonely men and women of the future. What you might not have known is that Galaxy Brides (formerly aka "Galaxy Alien Mail Order Brides") dabbled in taking grooms to destinations—namely Earth! Unfortunately, they found the alien males a little too hard to control once they landed on our surface.

I hope you have as much fun reading this series as I've had writing it!

Happy Reading!

Michelle M. Pillow

To My Readers,
For always being willing to take that next adventure
with me.

Not on the Planet of Zorveya

Solarestabinian wanted to go home. He needed sunlight, not the artificial light of the ship. Being trapped in the metal box lowered his energy levels, which in turn made him edgy.

He hadn't been this angry since the Tyoe invasion of the southern mines. At least then the enemy had been worthy of his rage, not this incompetent crew of intergalactic matchmakers who couldn't navigate their way out of a nebula.

Literally. The Galaxy Alien Mail Order Brides' crew had gotten lost in space more than once. If you could call Bob, Gary, and their trainee, Harris, a crew.

"I am a warrior of the Solarus Elite Guard," he growled, pacing the length of the spacecraft's cramped cabin. Golden sparks of light trailed his movements, causing the ship's electrical systems to flicker in response. "I am not a mate-seeker. This mission is beneath me."

Eclipsyionic, or Eclipse as their handlers insisted on calling him, sat calmly in the pilot's chair, watching as Harris fumbled with the controls of the landing pod. Bob and Gary had stayed behind on the main ship and gave them directives through the comms.

"The Peacemaker Council believes this diplomatic initiative is our best chance for preventing war," Eclipse said. He lived in the twilight area of their tidal locked planet, the space between the permanent daylight where Solar and his people resided, and the eternal night of the others.

"The council can take their initiative and shove it into a black hole," Solar grumbled, his skin pulsing brighter with his mounting frustration. A panel to his right began to smoke. "If they wanted peace, they should have sent actual diplomats, not a soldier and a shadow-crawler."

From the darkest corner of the ship, Luniaren, now called Lunar, spoke without emerging from the gloom. "For once, I agree with the light-bearer. This mission is a waste of resources."

"See?" Solar gestured toward the shadows. "Even the night-creeper agrees with me. This is a pointless exercise."

"Your cooperation is not optional," Eclipse reminded them both. "The contract has been signed. The council was quite clear about the consequences of failure. Now dim your light before you fry the system."

Solar's light dimmed slightly at the reminder. His council delegate had made their intent clear. Succeed in this absurd mission, or don't bother returning to Zorveya. He had family in the light zone, younger siblings who depended on his status as an Elite Guard. Exile was not an option.

"I refuse to mate with a primitive Earth female," he declared, though with less conviction than before.

"You don't have to mate," Eclipse clarified, not for the first time. "You simply need to demonstrate that you can peacefully coexist with humans and form a meaningful connection."

"Connection," Solar scoffed. "What sort of connection could I possibly form with a species that can't even harness their own star's energy properly?"

The ship lurched suddenly, throwing Solar

against a wall. His instinctive flare of defensive light caused three more control panels to short-circuit.

"Control your emissions!" Lunar hissed from his corner.

"Control your shadows!" Solar shot back, aware it wasn't his wittiest retort but too disoriented to care.

Eclipse sighed the sigh of someone who had been mediating the same argument for far too long. "We're entering Earth's atmosphere. Please secure yourselves."

"Chairs do not burn!" Harris announced cheerfully, as he pressed buttons seemingly at random. His malfunctioning translator had been a constant problem on the trip.

The ship began to shake violently. Solar grabbed a restraint strap as warning lights flashed across the cabin. Harris began hitting the ship's control panel, causing renewed tension in the cockpit. Through the viewscreen, he could see the surface of Earth rushing toward them at an alarming speed.

"Is this supposed to happen?" he asked, his golden skin pulsing with alarm. They pretended like they didn't hear him.

"Not to worry," Bob's chopped voice yelled over the comms. "This," the screen went black, "normal... worried," static, "first-time landings."

"Did he say crash landings?" Solar demanded, trying to keep his anger in check. He was so close to setting this ship on fire.

"First-time landings," Eclipse corrected.

Solar didn't believe him for a second.

"If we survive this," Solar vowed under his breath, "I'm going to melt Gary and Bob into puddles."

"Not if I freeze them first," Lunar muttered.

The comms went dead and Gary's voice stopped.

"We're coming in too fast," Lunar stated the obvious from his shadowed corner. "You should slow the ship."

"Do you think?" Solar resisted the urge to flare, but it was difficult. "I hadn't noticed with all the alarms."

Something was very wrong with their descent trajectory. The ship began to vibrate, which made it difficult to hear.

"What are the odds we will survive this impact?" Solar yelled over the noise.

"Pudding," Harris declared with the help of his malfunctioning translator. "We die like brides!"

"We're not brides," Solar shouted.

"If we survive," Lunar stated, "I really will kill Bob and Gary. Harris will die from his own ineptitude."

"Squish like pizza," Harris answered.

"Not if I get to them first," Solar swore, though he wasn't sure they'd survive long enough. This is not how a warrior was meant to die.

The alien tour guides kept talking, but Solar blocked their words as he tried to brace himself. They clipped a tall red rock formation, and a piece of the outer ship tore away. The impact sent them spinning wildly. Alarms blared louder, as if they didn't already know they were in trouble.

"Brace for impact!" Eclipse ordered.

The ship hit the surface hard, bouncing several times before skidding to a halt. Solar's restraints snapped, sending him crashing into the ceiling before he tumbled down onto Eclipse. Green smoke filled the cabin.

"Stop glowing," Lunar yelled. "You're making the systems worse."

The ship finally stopped. Solar illuminated a soft light from his place on the floor, trying to see in the darkness.

An automated voice announced, "Warning. Atmospheric seal compromised. Emergency protocols initiated."

Solar covered his mouth and tried not to breathe

in the smoke. This is not how he was going to die, in the dark on a foreign planet.

The ship creaked. Suddenly, the floor dropped out from beneath them.

Solar fell through the opening, landing with a heavy thud on Earth. His skin flared brightly in response to pain and disorientation, temporarily illuminating the area around him like a small sun. Something caught fire next to him. When his vision cleared, he saw Eclipse and Lunar picking themselves up nearby, while Harris lay face down, apparently unconscious.

"Magnificent arrival," Solar remarked sarcastically, rising to his feet. They had bounce-landed on top of a building, high above the surrounding landscape. "Truly, a grand entrance befitting honored representatives of Zorveya."

A loud creak sounded, and he turned just in time to see the crashed spaceship rolling on the collapsing rooftop toward them.

"Jump!" Eclipse ordered, grabbing Harris by the back of his clothing to carry him over the edge.

Lunar slithered off the side of the building seconds before he would have been crushed. Solar surged, emitting heat to push the ship back in the other direction. Fire erupted around him, and the spacecraft rolled over the side, crushing trees.

Solar walked away from the flames and glanced down at the ground. Harris stood, wobbling as Eclipse pulled him to safety. Solar leaned down, grabbed the edge, and leapt to the ground.

The roof blazed above.

"Welcome to Duskrock!" Gary's muffled voice greeted them with crackling cheer from the direction of the wreckage.

Before they could reply, Harris stood as if everything was normal and scuttled toward the wreckage.

"I detect a slight deviation from the planned landing zone, but nothing to worry about. The locals here are very receptive to unusual occurrences," Gary's voice continued, coming closer.

Harris returned, holding a comm and carrying a bag. He wore what appeared to be a hastily applied skin suit that made him look like a deformed Earth child.

"Quick, put on your skin suits," Gary's voice ordered as Harris thrust bundles of fabric into their arms. "They go under the maintenance worker uniforms. It's the perfect camouflage. No one will suspect."

"Extra pudding," Harris said as if agreeing with his boss.

Solar looked up. Smoke billowed from the structure. "This is too noticeable. We need to find shelter."

He reluctantly pulled the constrictive material of the skin suit over his glowing form, noting how the dull fabric dampened his natural radiance and blocked the sunlight from proper absorption. The uniform was ill-fitting, but it would have to do.

"What about our supplies?" he demanded.

"Slight complication there," Gary's voice admitted. "The cargo hold release malfunctioned, and the ship is on fire. But not to worry. We've arranged temporary accommodations at a local establishment called Crimson Rock Inn. Very prestigious. We'll retrieve your full provisions once we secure the ship."

"And how long will that take?" Eclipse asked.

Harris' smile never faltered as he continued to hold the comm emitting Gary's voice. "Hard to say. Hours? Days? The technical team is... well, Harris is the technical team, and he appears to require retraining."

Solar fought the urge to incinerate Harris on the spot. Only the approaching humans kept him from doing so. The gathering crowd pointed devices at the crash.

"They're recording us," Lunar observed quietly.

"Harris, take them in the right direction. Follow Harris," Gary instructed, as Harris carried the comm toward a gap between the trees and the building. "Stay casual. Blend in."

"Blend in?" Solar hissed, gesturing to his skin, which glowed visibly even through the uniform. "How, exactly, am I supposed to do that?"

"Just act natural," Gary suggested, unhelpfully. "Take the local currency in the bag Harris is providing. Get settled, while Bob and I will sort out the ship situation. Harris, give them the communicator, then secure the ship before we get there."

Harris handed the comm to Eclipse and waddled off. Solar exchanged a glance with Eclipse, who merely shrugged. Even Lunar seemed at a loss.

"I will not forget this humiliation," Solar promised as they slipped away from the crash site, ducking along the fiery structure labeled "Pete's Crystal Emporium."

A human female organizing the chaotic crowd called out to them. Eclipse stepped forward, turning toward her with an expression Solar had never seen on the diplomat's face before. Perhaps Eclipse wasn't as immune to primitive attractions as he claimed. Now was not the time for this. Then again, the skin suit made it hard to decipher expressions.

Before they could interact, another human female pulled the first one away, and Solar urgently herded them in the opposite direction.

"Crimson Rock Inn is forward toward the blue tower," Gary's voice insisted.

"And where exactly are you and Bob?" Lunar asked suspiciously.

"Managing the crisis from a strategic location," Gary answered.

"Hiding," Solar translated.

"Strategic location," Gary corrected. "Not to worry. Harris is onworld with you. Now, a reminder about your Earth names. You'll need to use them at all times in public."

"We discussed this already," Solar growled. "I refuse to be called Solar Bound."

"But it's perfect," Gary protested. "Solar is a common Earth name, and Bound suggests you're strong and powerful like a, uh, rivet. Plus, it's memorable."

Solar didn't bother explaining that on Zorveya, "bound" was slang for someone caught pleasuring themselves while trapped in a vine patch. His new designation was both humiliating and inaccurate. He had never been *bound* in his life and had no intention of starting now.

"I vote we throw him and find our own way," Lunar suggested.

Eclipse pulled the comm closer and shook his head.

Gary gave them directions and guided them through the streets. Solar couldn't help noticing how bright everything was. The sun here was weaker than on Zorveya, but it bathed the landscape in a pleasant golden glow that reminded him of home. Anything was better than the ship hull. The humans barely glanced at them, too busy with their own activities to notice three aliens in maintenance uniforms.

"What kind of creature is that?" Lunar asked, gesturing to a figure in a silver suit with a lizard head.

Eclipse frowned. "Biosignature says Earth human."

"He has an unfortunate face," Solar observed.

"It is a biological female," Eclipse corrected.

"Here we are," Gary announced, stopping them in front of a two-story building with a sign depicting a large red rock. "Your temporary home until we can arrange more suitable accommodations."

The prestigious Crimson Rock Inn turned out to

be a basic shelter with primitive amenities. Eclipse made them hide as he went to procure keys. He then led them to a room with two beds, which Solar would apparently be sharing with Eclipse and Lunar.

"One room?" he demanded, sparks flying from his fingertips. "For all three of us? This is worse than the ship."

"We're lucky to have it. They were at capacity until Bob destroyed the transport of a gigolo from California," Gary explained with a nervous laugh. "But look at the bright side, you'll have plenty of opportunity to practice peaceful coexistence. Won't that be exciting?"

"Gigolo is a better name than bound. It sounds regal. I will be Solar Gigolo."

"Stop grumbling," Eclipse snapped. "Our Earth papers say Bound. Do not make things more difficult."

Solar's skin flared so brightly that Lunar had to shield his eyes.

"Bob and I will check in tomorrow with more details about your mission. There's currency in the bag for necessities, and a pamphlet reminder about local customs. Remember, your objective is to blend in, observe humans, and identify potential compatible mates. Exciting, right?" the alien matchmaker said. "I'll let you get settled."

"A good mating would probably help that one's temper, he's what the humans call a pain in the..." Bob's voice sounded far away, and Solar was sure that it wasn't meant for their ears.

"Wait," Eclipse tried to stop Gary from signing off, but the comm went dead.

Solar frowned, surveying the cramped room with disgust. "You should have let me incinerate him when we had the chance. This is intolerable. I refuse to share sleeping quarters with a shadow-dweller."

"The feeling is mutual, light-leaker," Lunar replied coolly from the darkest corner.

Eclipse positioned himself between them, as usual. "We need to make the best of this situation. The sooner we complete our mission objectives, the sooner we can return home."

"And how exactly are we supposed to find compatible mates in this primitive settlement?" Solar demanded. "The lizard head might be Lunar's type, but—"

"I will snuff you and leave your pile of ash in the desert for them to autopsy," Lunar warned. "Then you won't have to worry about a ride home."

"Mates are not our immediate concern," Eclipse

replied. "First, we need to adapt to Earth customs and establish our cover identities. The mating aspect can wait."

Solar snorted. "Easy for you to say. You've already found your biorhythm match."

Eclipse's expression remained neutral, but Solar didn't miss the slight change in his energy pattern. "I don't know what you mean."

"The female at the crash site," Solar pressed. "The one organizing the humans."

"Your energy signature fluctuated when she spoke," Lunar added. "I felt it."

"That's irrelevant," Eclipse said firmly. "Our mission—"

"Is a farce," Solar interrupted, "but if we must participate in this charade, I intend to excel at it. I will find the most compatible, most impressive Earth female and form a connection so meaningful it will make the council regret ever doubting me."

"This isn't a competition," Eclipse sighed.

Wrong. To Solar, everything was a competition. And he never, ever lost.

He moved to the window, pulling aside the flimsy fabric covering to let more sunlight in. Lunar immediately hissed in discomfort, retreating further into his corner.

"Turn that down," the shadow-dweller commanded.

"Make me," Solar challenged, absorbing the sunlight with deliberate showiness. His skin brightened, and the room's electronic devices began to flicker in response to his energy output.

"Both of you, stop," Eclipse ordered. "This behavior is exactly why we're here."

Solar ignored him, focusing instead on the view outside. Humans moved about their business, oblivious to the three extraterrestrials observing them. They seemed so fragile, so unaware. How could any of them possibly be a match for him, Solarestabinian of the Elite Guard?

Then he spotted her, a female with hair the color of flames, moving with a grace that belied her species' general clumsiness. She was performing some kind of ritual in an open space near the building, spinning objects that trailed fire through the air.

For the first time since landing on this primitive planet, Solar felt a flicker of genuine interest.

"Perhaps this mission won't be a complete waste after all," he murmured, watching as the fire-spinner executed a complex maneuver that sent spirals of flame dancing around her body.

Eclipse followed his gaze. "Solar, whatever you're thinking... Don't."

But Solar was already formulating a plan. She resonated with his energy signature in an unexpected way. If he had to find an Earth female to connect with, it might as well be one who understood the power and beauty of fire energy.

Solar smiled, his skin pulsing with renewed energy. Earth might be primitive, and this mission might be beneath him, but he was a warrior.

And warriors always found a way to triumph.

2

CRIMSON ROCK INN, DUSKROCK, ARIZONA

Solar hated Earth sleeping platforms. The soft, yielding material provided inadequate thermal contact for proper energy transfer. He'd spent the night cycle tossing on the lumpy surface, unable to achieve proper regenerative stillness. The constant hum of Earth devices didn't help, nor did Lunar's occasional shadow manipulations from his makeshift nest in the human bathing chamber. Thankfully, his roommate had disappeared into the night and had yet to return.

Nighttime was like being locked in a shadowland prison.

When Earth's sun finally appeared, Solar positioned himself by the window, absorbing what meager rays made it through the transparent barrier. The radiation here was weaker than on Zorveya, having been filtered through a thicker atmosphere and emanating from a less powerful star. Still, it was better than the oppressive darkness of space travel.

His skin tingled as it absorbed the sunlight, golden particles activating beneath the surface. Much better. Now, if only the primitive dwelling had proper nutrition. The continental breakfast mentioned on the information card had proven disappointing, consisting primarily of carbohydrate-rich substances with minimal energy content, called cinnamon rolls and bagels.

Eclipse had gone out in the night to make contact with the human female he'd shown interest in at the landing site. His energy stone indicated she controlled accommodations that were much better suited to their needs. Solar would have protested the exposure, but he needed out of the quarters shared with Lunar.

Eclipse had left them again to meet with the woman. He said her name was Rowan. Strange, but then anything was better than Bound. Solar had doubts about trusting a primitive species with matters of interplanetary diplomacy, but Eclipse seemed unusually invested in this particular human.

"Her biorhythms are calm," Eclipse had explained, as if that justified everything. "We can trust her."

Solar understood the concept. Even he had felt an unexpected resonance with the fire-manipulating female he'd observed yesterday. But that didn't mean he was ready to form a meaningful connection with an underdeveloped species. He was a warrior of the Solarus Elite Guard, not some desperate lunar shadow crawler seeking companionship in dark corners.

Speaking of which, Lunar had vanished during the night and still hadn't returned. Probably skulking around, terrifying the locals with his creeping shadow routine. Or worse, making contact with potential mates without proper protocols.

Not that Solar cared. If the shadow dweller wanted to fail the mission by traumatizing Earth females, that was his problem.

Solar straightened, feeling his energy levels finally reaching acceptable parameters. Time to begin his own reconnaissance. If he were stuck on this planet for a month, he might as well gather useful intelligence. And perhaps locate that flame-haired female again.

For mission purposes, of course.

He examined the Earth garments Eclipse had purchased for them to blend in. Crude fabrics in drab colors, designed for functionality rather than status display. No sign of rank insignia or house markings. How did humans identify their social hierarchies without proper attire indicators?

Solar selected the least offensive garments—a dark covering for his lower extremities, known as jeans, and an upper body wrap in golden hues that complemented his coloration. The skin-suit went on first, dampening his natural luminescence to levels that wouldn't immediately reveal his extraterrestrial origins. He hated the sensation, like being wrapped in wet sand, but accepted the necessity.

The final look was tolerable, if undignified. He looked like a low-ranking maintenance worker rather than an Elite Guard, but at least the shirt mimicked some of his natural radiance that wasn't allowed to shine through.

Solar consulted the information device Eclipse had left. It contained primitive maps of the settlement and instructions for accessing the local currency system. According to the device, the area called "Uptown Duskrock" contained the highest concentration of social gathering places and commercial establishments. A logical place to begin his search.

The corridors of Crimson Rock Inn were quiet as Solar made his way toward the exit. Most humans were apparently still engaged in their sleep cycle, despite the sun having risen.

Inefficient creatures.

Outside, the morning air was cool but pleasant. The distinctive red rock formations glowed in the early sunlight, their mineral composition creating interesting energy patterns that Solar's enhanced perception could detect. At least this planet had interesting geology, if nothing else to recommend it.

He followed the information device's directions, moving with purpose toward the commercial district. Humans he passed gave him curious glances, but didn't seem alarmed by his presence. Perhaps Gary and Bob had been right about this settlement being accustomed to unusual visitors.

Solar absorbed the unfamiliar sights and sounds, cataloging them for later analysis. He felt a pull of energy and naturally followed it. Earth vehicles rumbled along paved pathways. Strange flying creatures made repetitive noise patterns. Humans consumed liquid stimulants at outdoor tables. All were so primitive, yet functioning in their own limited way.

A sudden flare of energy caught his attention. Across an open area came a flash of familiar movement. The fire-manipulating female from yesterday was setting up some kind of display. Her distinctive red hair shone in the sunlight, and her actions had the same fluid grace that had first caught his attention.

Solar changed course immediately, drawn toward this potential source of compatible energy. As he approached, he could see she was arranging metallic objects on a cloth covering. Small implements that gleamed in the sunlight, alongside the fire-spinning tools he'd observed her using before.

The female looked up as he approached, her eyes a unique green color. They narrowed slightly. "Can I help you?"

Her voice had a pleasant resonance frequency. Solar felt his own energy signature responding, his skin brightening beneath the restrictive skin-suit.

"I observed your fire manipulation yesterday," he stated, seeing no reason for deception. "It was adequate."

The female's expression shifted, her mouth tightening. "Gee, thanks, mister. Always nice to hear my art is adequate."

Solar frowned. Had he used the wrong Earth term? His translator should have selected an appropriate descriptive.

"Your technical execution exceeded basic competency parameters," he clarified.

The female stared at him for a moment, then laughed. The sound created interesting harmonic vibrations in the air between them.

"You're either the worst flirt I've ever met or you're not from around here," she said, returning to arranging her implements. "Either way, I'm busy setting up."

"I am not from around here," Solar confirmed, stepping closer to examine her tools. "These are your flame projection devices?"

She glanced up again, studying him more carefully this time. "Yeah. Fire poi, staffs, fans. I do performances at the Crash Zone on weekends, and I sell handmade fire tools here during the day."

"You create these implements yourself?" Solar was genuinely impressed. Manual crafting was rare on Zorveya, where most items were produced through automated molecular assembly.

"Every single one." Pride entered her voice. "I'm Dani, by the way. Dani Ember."

"Em-ber," Solar repeated, recognizing the term from his Earth language data packet. "A particle of fire that remains after the main combustion event. An appropriate designation."

Dani tilted her head, her green eyes narrowing again. "And you are...?"

"Solar Bound," he replied, using his humiliating Earth name despite his distaste for it. He waited to see if she'd recoil.

"Solar," she repeated, a smile forming. "Let me guess, you're one of those performance artists from Burning Man? Here for the vortex festival?"

Solar wasn't sure what burning men or vortex festivals entailed, but he recognized an opportunity when it presented itself.

"Yes," he agreed. "I am very interested in fire manipulation techniques. Perhaps you could demonstrate your methods."

Dani's smile widened. "I don't usually do private lessons, but you caught me in a good mood. I'm doing a fire dance at the Crash Zone tonight. Come by around nine, and if you're genuinely interested, I'll show you some basics after my set."

Solar felt a surge of satisfaction. First contact

established, further interaction arranged. His mission was progressing more efficiently than Eclipse's diplomatic fumbling or Lunar's shadow lurking.

"I will come to this Crash Zone at the designated time," he confirmed.

"Great," Dani said, turning her attention back to her display. "Now, if you don't mind, I need to finish setting up before the tourists arrive."

Solar recognized the dismissal but found himself reluctant to leave. Something about this human's energy signature called to his own in a way he hadn't anticipated. Her manipulation of fire indicated an affinity for light and heat that most Earth creatures seemed to lack.

Perhaps this mission wasn't entirely pointless after all.

"Until tonight," he said, stepping back. "Your fire demonstration will be impressive, I'm certain."

Dani looked up one last time, her expression unreadable. "We'll see if you still think so after you've watched me perform."

Solar turned and continued his exploration of the commercial district, but his thoughts remained fixed on the fire-manipulator and their upcoming interaction. This Crash Zone would provide an opportunity to observe human mating behaviors in their natural setting, while also studying this planet's advanced fire manipulation techniques.

And if Dani Ember's biorhythms proved as compatible as his initial readings suggested, perhaps he could complete the meaningful connection portion of his mission sooner than expected.

As he walked, Solar noticed his skin was glowing more brightly beneath the skin-suit. Tiny motes of golden light escaped around the edges. He forced himself to dampen his emissions, though it went against his natural instincts. On Zorveya, a warrior proudly displayed his light, especially when approaching a potential mate.

These Earth protocols were frustratingly restrictive. How would she know to accept his offer if she couldn't see its immense glow?

A loud commotion drew his attention. Humans had gathered around a street performer, an elderly male wearing elaborate ceremonial garments decorated with feathers and beads. Now, this was a man who knew how to dress. The performer was speaking loudly about ancient alien visitors and celestial wisdom.

Solar moved closer, curious about these claims of extraterrestrial contact.

"The star people have always come to guide us,"

the human said, his voice carrying across the gathering. "They taught my ancestors the secrets of the universe, and they walk among us still, watching, waiting for the right moment to reveal themselves once more."

Several humans in the crowd nodded in agreement, while others exchanged skeptical glances. Solar found the entire scene fascinating. These humans seemed to simultaneously believe in and doubt the existence of extraterrestrial intelligence. How did they function with such cognitive dissonance?

The street performer spotted Solar and fixed him with an intense stare. "You! I sense cosmic energy in you, brother. Come forward and let the crowd feel your vibrations."

Solar froze. Had his skin-suit malfunctioned? Was his natural luminescence visible to this perceptive human?

Before he could retreat, the performer grabbed his arm and pulled him into the center of the gathering. "See how he glows with inner light. This one understands the star wisdom!"

The crowd murmured with interest. Several humans pointed recording devices at him. Solar felt his fight-or-flight response activating. If his true nature were exposed, the mission would be compromised.

"I must go," he said firmly, pulling his arm free.

"The star people are shy," the performer declared. "They hide their true nature until we are ready to receive their full glory."

Solar backed away from the gathering, keeping his head down and his emissions tightly controlled. This was exactly the kind of attention Eclipse had warned them to avoid. If the footage of him spread through Earth's primitive information networks, their cover could be blown.

He needed to find a less conspicuous location to continue his reconnaissance. According to the information device, there was a place called Alien Arts Village nearby. Perhaps there he could blend in more effectively among the commercial activities.

As Solar made his way toward this new destination, he couldn't help reflecting on the irony of the situation. The elderly human had been correct about aliens walking among the crowds, yet his theatrical presentation had made the truth seem like an absurd performance.

Earth was turning out to be more complex than he'd anticipated. Their primitive technology and chaotic social structures masked surprising insights and perceptions. And some individuals, like the fire manipulator Dani, displayed capabilities that hinted at a greater potential than their species' overall development level would suggest.

Tonight's interaction at the Crash Zone would provide more data. And perhaps, though Solar was reluctant to admit it even to himself, something more than mere mission objectives.

The thought of watching Dani dance with fire created a pleasant resonance. Yes, this investigation warranted his personal attention. After all, he was a warrior of the Solarus Elite Guard. And warriors always pursued their objectives with unwavering focus, even when those objectives involved fiery Earth females with challenging attitudes and intriguing energy signatures.

3

Fire had rules. Rules Dani had spent years learning, respecting, and occasionally bending just enough to make it dance. Fire demanded precision. Focus. Respect. Three things most people in her life had never given her.

"Hey, firegirl!" Mike, the bar owner, called from behind the counter as Dani hauled her equipment through the back door of The Crash Zone. "You're early."

"Need to set up," she answered, dropping her duffel bag beside the small stage area. "The rig needs adjusting after last week's close call."

Mike winced. "Yeah, don't need another singed eyebrow situation. Bad for business."

"Bad for my face," Dani corrected, pulling out her

tools. The ceiling rig needed reinforcing, and she wasn't about to trust anyone else to do it. Too many fire performers trusted their safety to others. Dani trusted herself, her tools, and the fire. Nothing else.

The Crash Zone was still quiet this early, hours before the Friday night UFO enthusiast crowd would descend with their tinfoil hats and wild theories. Dani preferred it this way, just her and the muffled sounds of Mike stocking the bar, the occasional clink of bottles like a comforting metronome as she worked.

Her performance area was a circular clearing in the center of the bar, surrounded by tables set at a safe distance. Above it hung her custom-designed rig. It was a series of reinforced anchor points that allowed her to suspend various fire props for the more impressive parts of her routine. It wasn't fancy, but it was functional, and more importantly, it was hers.

As she climbed the stepladder to reach the ceiling mounts, Dani's mind wandered to the strange man from that morning. Solar. What kind of name was that? Probably some stage name for yet another Burning Man performer thinking they could waltz into Duskrock and claim territory.

But there had been something different about

him. The way he'd studied her fire tools with genuine curiosity, not the fake interest she got from guys trying to hit on her. And those strange compliments, *"your technical execution exceeded basic competency parameters."* Who talked like that?

The memory made her smile despite herself. There was something almost endearing about his awkwardness. And he was undeniably attractive, with that golden skin that seemed to shimmer in the sunlight. Probably some kind of specialty bronzer, though she hadn't been able to spot any application lines or smudges on his clothing.

"Thinking about a guy?" Mike asked, startling her.

Dani nearly dropped her wrench. "Jesus, Mike! Don't sneak up on someone on a ladder."

"Wasn't sneaking. You were zoned out, smiling like you won the lottery."

"Just thinking about new routines," she lied, tightening the last bolt with more force than necessary. "I'm adding the double fire fans tonight."

Mike whistled. "The ones with the extended wicks? Impressive. Just don't burn my ceiling down."

"Fifteen years of performances, never burned down a venue," Dani reminded him, climbing down. "You're not going to be my first."

"Better not be. My guy told me insurance premiums are going up again after that UFO thing yesterday. Everyone's claiming property damage."

Dani had been at her stall when it happened. There had been a bright object streaking across the sky, followed by a distant crash. The tourists loved it, of course. UFO sightings were good for business. She'd sold three fire staffs to excited visitors convinced aliens had arrived, and one to a guy looking to defend himself. Him, she gave a toy model. She would not be responsible for him setting something on fire.

"Did you see it?" Mike asked, following her back to her equipment.

"The UFO? Hard to miss."

"No, the video going around. Someone at the crystal shop captured footage of three men walking away from the crash site. One of them was glowing."

Dani rolled her eyes. "Glowing? Seriously?"

"I'm telling you, it's freaky. Face was kind of blurred, but the dude had this golden shimmer thing going on."

That made Dani pause in unpacking her fire poi. Golden shimmer. Like Solar's skin in the sunlight.

"Probably just lens flare," she said, dismissing the thought. Duskrock attracted all types, and she'd long ago stopped trying to separate the genuinely strange from the attention-seeking weird.

"Maybe. But my buddy at Crimson Rock Inn says they got three new guests yesterday, no luggage, paid in cash, weird accents. And one of them keeps making the lights flicker."

"Your buddy also believes his ex was abducted by aliens when she just moved to Phoenix."

Mike laughed. "Fair point. Anyway, we're expecting a full house tonight. UFO sighting always brings out the crowds."

"Good. I need the tips." Dani pulled out her fuel bottles, carefully arranging them on her prep table. "I'm behind on rent again."

"You know, you could pick up some bartending shifts. I've offered."

"And risk these hands?" She held up her calloused but graceful fingers. "These are precision instruments, Mike. I'm not risking cuts from your cheap well tequila."

The truth was, Dani had tried normal jobs. They never stuck. Something about punching a clock and answering to people who didn't understand her made her feel like she was suffocating. Fire was freedom. When she danced with flame, she belonged to no one but herself.

She'd come to Duskrock five years ago with nothing but her fire tools and enough money for one month's rent. It wasn't the first fresh start she'd attempted, but something about this place had held her. The red rocks. The open sky. The way people here accepted the unusual as part of daily life.

It wasn't perfect. The rent was too high, the tourists could be annoying, and the locals were divided between genuine spiritual seekers and opportunistic crystal hawkers... but it was home. For now, at least.

"Earth to Dani," Mike waved a hand in front of her face. "You keep zoning out. You okay?"

"Fine," she said. "Just mentally choreographing."

"Well, choreograph while you help me move these tables. I want to expand your performance space a bit."

As they rearranged the furniture, Dani found herself wondering if Solar would actually show up tonight. Part of her hoped he would. It had been a while since anyone had piqued her curiosity. Most men either found her intimidating or fetishized her fire dancing in ways that made her skin crawl.

Solar had seemed different. There was an intensity to him that matched her own, a focus she rarely saw in others. And when he'd watched her arrange her tools, his eyes had followed her movements with something like recognition, as if he understood what it meant to channel and control energy.

"You're doing it again," Mike pointed out, snapping his fingers in front of her face.

"Doing what?"

"The smile. Definitely a guy."

"Shut up and move the table, Mike."

4

———

Solar detected Lunar's distinct energy patterns and followed him to keep an eye on the shadow-dweller, which was not how he had planned to spend his time on this primitive planet. He was not what Earth people called a person who sat on babies, but he would also not let his mission be ruined when he was so close to completing his agenda in record time.

"Let him go," he had told Eclipse last night after Lunar departed from their inadequate Crimson Rock dwelling. "Maybe he'll find a cave to hide in."

However, when Lunar failed to return, Eclipse had insisted that they locate him.

"The mission requires all three of us to remain in

proximity," he'd said with that irritating diplomatic tone. "We cannot afford to lose track of each other."

Solar had drawn the short metallic rod, which apparently meant he was responsible for locating their missing shadow-dweller while Eclipse met with his human female to secure better accommodations. The Earth custom of determining duties through random chance seemed inefficient, but Solar wasn't about to question it while Eclipse's attention was elsewhere.

Tracking Lunar wasn't a challenge. The shadow-dweller left a distinctive energy signature. The cold void disrupted natural light patterns. Solar could sense these disruptions with his enhanced perception, following the trail like footprints across the settlement.

The path led to a large complex nestled among the red rocks, identified by Earth signage as the Duskrock Yoga and Spa Meditation Center. The retreat's parking area was filled with vehicles, and humans moved about in strange, loose-fitting attire. Many carried thin mats rolled under their arms. He recognized the location from the spinning viewing screen when they crashed. This was also where Eclipse said their new dwelling would be located.

Perhaps Lunar was with him, and Solar could end his hunt.

Solar's skin-suit felt increasingly restrictive as Earth's sun climbed higher. The dampening effect on his natural light was necessary for blending in, but uncomfortable. Like trying to contain a star in a paper bag. Small sparks occasionally escaped around his wrists and collar, forcing him to readjust the membrane.

He approached the main building, noting that the security was minimal. A human male at the entrance barely glanced at him before returning to his overlord communication device. Solar strode past as if he belonged there, projecting the confidence befitting a Solarus Elite Guard.

Inside, the air smelled of burning plants. Humans sat in circular formations in several rooms, contorting their bodies into unnatural positions. His energy could easily mimic such actions, but humans had a solid foundation. Was this some form of ritual-istic torture? Or perhaps preparation for combat? He had been doubting whether the Earth population was ready for a fight should one come.

He detected Lunar's energy signature growing stronger, coming from deeper within the building. At the same time, he sensed Eclipse's presence nearby.

Solar moved through the corridors, ignoring the curious glances from passing humans. His height and build made him stand out even with the skin-suit concealing his true nature. One female dressed in white fabrics approached him with a serene smile.

"Are you here for the cosmic alignment meditation?" she asked. "It's about to start in the Crystal Room."

"No," Solar replied curtly. "I am tracking a shadow-dweller."

The female's smile didn't falter. "A shadow worker? For energy clearance? That would be down the east hall, past the sound bath."

Earth females were strange in their interpretations. Solar nodded and continued in the direction she indicated, which happened to align with Lunar's energy signature.

As he rounded a corner, he felt a sudden surge in electromagnetic activity. The lights in the corridor flickered wildly, and a small decorative fountain ceased functioning. Solar recognized the pattern. Lunar was actively manipulating shadows, something he only did when agitated or threatened.

"I know you've been following me, show yourself," a woman demanded loudly.

Solar frowned and stopped to listen.

The shadows darkened their way down the hall, crawling toward him. Such obvious shadow play was abnormal for Lunar. Something more was happening. Had Lunar also found a female to pursue? And in doing so, had he started a conflict? It was the only logical conclusion. What female would want a shadow after her? Humans feared the darkness. And with good cause. Nothing good came from the dark.

Solar turned directions and hurried to find Eclipse. If Lunar had stumbled into a battle, logic said they'd be stronger as a trio. The lights flickered, partially due to his agitation and partially because Lunar was dampening the building's power. Their conflicting energy signatures played havoc on Earth's power grids.

He'd be lying if he said the idea of a fight didn't excite him. He was a man of action. All this hiding and stealth went against his very nature.

Solar opened a door. Sparks came off his hand, and he stated without fully examining the room, "Eclipse, come. We have a problem. Lunar is skulking, and I believe he's tracking a human female."

"You're glowing," a female with Eclipse whispered. Rowan, Eclipse had called her.

Solar hadn't detected her before now. Probably because she hummed with Eclipse's energy signature. What exactly had he walked in on? And why did the idea of transferring energy make him want to abandon his travel companions and find Dani?

Solar glanced at her but spoke toward Eclipse, "I see you have located your woman with the compatible biorhythms. She seems adequate."

"Solar," Eclipse scolded, as he was wont to do. "We discussed proper Earth protocols."

"Yes, yes. Don't call humans inadequate to their faces. I remember. I said she is adequate." Solar focused his energy on not overloading the electrical system. His translator insisted adequate was a complimentary word for these situations, but Dani had given him the same negative response. "But we have more pressing issues. Lunar is displaying signs of possible mate fixation on a loud female, and if he follows his instincts, he may—"

"He wouldn't harm her," Eclipse insisted, defending Lunar like usual.

"Of course not," Solar scoffed. "But he might be attempting communication, which would be far worse. You know how he gets. All shadows and cryptic statements. Humans find it unsettling. I have seen references in their horror movies. They will try to exercise him."

Solar noted the brief flicker of surprise on the woman's face. "Exercise? I think you mean exorcise."

"Yes." Solar felt sparks escaping his suit in agitation. This was not a productive conversation.

"You really are aliens," she said.

Eclipse gave a small gesture to indicate Solar should calm his aggressions. Interesting. Perhaps their leader's interest in this human went deeper than mission necessity.

Solar turned to her and tried to smile. She shielded her eyes at the bright light that escaped his mouth hole. "Of course we are. Did Eclipse not explain properly? Galaxy Alien Mail Order Brides sent us to your primitive planet to find mates and prevent an interplanetary war. Though why anyone would want to mate with a species that can't even regulate their own bioelectricity is beyond me. No offense."

"Solar," Eclipse interrupted. "Find Lunar. Now. Before he causes a diplomatic incident."

Solar started to leave. It was clear that Eclipse was not readily coming with him. Fine. He'd handle the problem himself. Like always.

"Wait," Rowan demanded. "You can't keep walking around the retreat like that. I have a suite put aside for you. It's private."

"Find him and then find the suite. Stay out of sight," Eclipse said.

Solar left and quickened his pace as he entered the growing shadow. Within the darkness, he could hear voices. One was distinctly human and female, the other the cold tones of Lunar.

"I'm an anomaly," the female was saying. "The stone I gave you last night, did it help?"

"It's not safe for you to know about me," Lunar replied, his voice barely audible.

"I can't help who I am," the female insisted. "You can trust me."

Solar had heard enough. Eclipse doing it was one thing. At least the twilight-dweller had some sense. But if Lunar had exposed their true nature to a random human female, the entire mission could be compromised. He pushed open the door without warning, golden light spilling from his skin as his control slipped.

The room was small, filled with supplies and strange Earth food delivering artifacts that reminded him of the continental breakfast buffet. Lunar stood in the darkest corner, his true form partially visible as the skin-suit struggled to contain his shadow manipulation. Before him stood a human female with unusual coloration. Her hair was the shade of a long-dead star, and her eyes looked like Earth's twilight.

Both turned at his entrance, Lunar's expression darkening further while the female's eyes widened in recognition. The room was dark, except for the sunlight coming in through the window. Solar automatically amplified the light to fight the shadows.

"You," she whispered. "You're the bright one. From the crash."

Solar focused on Lunar, ignoring the female in his irritation about being outed. "Eclipse sent me. We must go to our assigned dwelling. You should not be talking to anyone."

"This human has unusual perceptive abilities," Lunar replied. "She detected my presence despite shadow concealment."

"That doesn't matter." Solar brightened with frustration. The room's lighting fixtures began to flicker and buzz. He didn't trust Lunar to make decisions regarding group safety. "Eclipse has secured new accommodations."

"The shadow stones should help," the female said to Lunar, seeming unfazed by Solar's display. "I have more if you need them."

Solar's attention snapped to her. "What do you know of us?"

The woman met his gaze without flinching. "I know you're not from here. I know you crashed near Pete's shop yesterday. I know you're different from each other, light and shadow." She gestured to the space around them. "And I know you can manipulate energy to the point you're disrupting the retreat's electrical system."

As if to emphasize her point, the overhead light exploded in a shower of sparks. She gave a small cry of surprise and moved out of the way.

"Poppy has offered assistance," Lunar said.

"Poppy?" Solar repeated, the Earth name strange on his tongue. "You revealed yourself to a human without authorization. Have you forgotten our mission parameters?"

"I revealed nothing," Lunar countered. "She perceived me through means I have yet to determine."

The female stepped forward. "Look, I don't want to cause trouble. I just want to help. Duskrock can be overwhelming for sensitive beings."

"We do not require your assistance," Solar said firmly. "And I am not sensitive."

Poppy raised an eyebrow. "Really? Because from where I'm standing, you two can barely be in the same room without causing electrical failures.

That seems like something that might draw attention."

The room's temperature seemed to drop several degrees as Lunar's shadows deepened. Simultaneously, Solar felt his own energy rising in response, his skin brightening against his will. The remaining lights in the room began to pulse erratically.

Eclipse charged into the room. "Both of you, control yourselves. You're causing an outage."

"I tracked the shadow-dweller as instructed," Solar replied. "He was engaged in unauthorized contact with this human."

"I was conducting necessary reconnaissance," Lunar argued.

Eclipse turned to Poppy.

"Hi. I'm Poppy Jensen. I work at Desert Animal Rescue," she said. "I felt your arrival yesterday. I gave your friend here a shadow stone last night when I sensed him outside The Crash Zone."

Solar glared at Lunar. "You attended the human gathering place without informing us and made contact?"

Yes, it was a double standard, but then again... This was *Lunar*.

"I was not aware I needed permission to conduct independent exploration," Lunar replied coldly.

"I have a suite reserved for you," Rowan said quickly. "Private entrance, separate bedrooms, minimal staff interaction. But we need to get you there now before someone calls the electrical company about the power surges."

"You trust this human?" Lunar demanded of Eclipse.

"You can call me Rowan." Eclipse's woman pointed at herself.

"Yes," Eclipse replied without hesitation.

"Fine," Solar stated, determining a relocation would be best for all. "Lead us to this suite."

"I wish to speak further with Poppy," Lunar said, not as a request but as a fact.

"You can do so later," Eclipse said firmly. "After we've relocated to a more secure area."

Poppy reached into a pocket and pulled out a small black stone, similar to the one Solar had seen Lunar examining at Crimson Rock Inn. She offered it to Solar.

"Black tourmaline," she explained. "It absorbs negative energy. You might find it helpful for dampening your output."

Solar hesitated, then accepted the stone. It felt cool in his palm, subtly drawing excess energy from his fingertips where the skin-suit had worn thin.

Curious, and a little unpleasant, like walking into Lunaris territory.

"We need to go now," Rowan insisted, glancing nervously at the door. "Stephanie just texted me. The maintenance crew is heading this way to check the electrical panel."

Eclipse nodded. "Solar, Lunar, follow us. And please, try to maintain your human appearance."

As they traveled through the corridor, Solar noticed Poppy falling into step beside Lunar, maintaining a respectful distance but clearly intending to accompany them. The shadow-dweller made no move to dismiss her.

Their strange procession moved through the retreat, Eclipse and Rowan leading the way, with Solar following closely behind. Lunar and Poppy brought up the rear, moving through deeper shadows along the walls.

"This way," Rowan directed them down a service corridor and through a door that led outside. "The Desert Suite is separate from the main buildings. It has its own generator backup if needed."

Solar blinked in the bright sunlight, absorbing the radiation.

"The suite was originally designed for celebrity

guests who wanted privacy," Rowan explained as they walked along a stone path.

"Your terms?" Solar asked, wondering why this female would help them.

"I used the cash you gave me and paid for a week upfront," she replied. "If anyone asks, you're listed under the Eclipse Group."

They approached a low structure built into the red rock, its design allowing it to blend almost seamlessly with the natural landscape. Solar had to admit it was an improvement over Crimson Rock Inn, particularly when Rowan unlocked the door to reveal spacious interiors with separate areas of light and shadow.

"The east-facing room gets morning sun," Rowan said, glancing at Solar. "The west room stays shaded most of the day and has blackout curtains," she added, nodding to Lunar. "And the center room has adjustable lighting."

Perfect for their respective biological needs. Perhaps this human was more perceptive than Solar had given her credit for.

"I'll leave you to get settled," Rowan said, placing a set of keys on a table. "There's a private entrance code for the gate. No one will disturb you here."

"I should go as well," Poppy said, glancing at

Lunar. "But I'd like to bring you something tomorrow. A proper welcome basket."

"That would be acceptable," Lunar replied before either Eclipse or Solar could object.

"Convenient that you've both found humans who accept our true nature so readily," Solar observed with suspicion once the females left. "While I alone maintain mission protocol."

Dani, of course, was a completely different scenario. He'd approached her but didn't tell her he was from outer space.

"Your light emissions are hardly maintaining protocol," Lunar pointed out. "You've damaged electronics in two separate locations now that we know of."

Solar felt his skin warming with irritation. "At least I'm not lurking in food holding chambers with random Earth females."

"Enough," Eclipse interjected. "We have suitable accommodations now. We should focus on the next phase of our mission."

"Finding mates," Solar stated flatly. "Although it seems you two have already begun that process."

"I have no interest in mating with Poppy," Lunar said, though Solar noted a slight shift in his shadow pattern that suggested uncertainty. "Her perceptive abilities simply warrant investigation."

"And Rowan is merely facilitating our mission," Eclipse added, a little too quickly.

Solar moved to the east-facing windows, where sunlight streamed in unobstructed. He absorbed the radiation, feeling his energy reserves replenishing. The room assignments were logical. Light for him, darkness for Lunar, and the balanced middle for Eclipse. Just like their home world.

He missed home. He missed the energy of his people.

"I think you're envious because you have not had a female show interest," Lunar said.

He instantly thought of Dani.

"I have an engagement tonight," Solar answered. "At The Crash Zone."

"With whom?" Eclipse asked.

"A fire manipulator," Solar replied, "who demonstrates flame control techniques that may be useful for our understanding of Earth combat capabilities. If we are trapped here, we will need to defend ourselves."

"Her name?" Lunar asked, a hint of amusement in his cold voice.

Solar hesitated. "Dani Ember."

Eclipse raised an eyebrow.

"It's research," Solar protested. "Unlike you two, I haven't forgotten why we're here."

Eclipse sighed. "Be careful. And try not to cause any more disturbances."

Solar turned back to the window, allowing the conversation to end. His interest in Dani's fire manipulation was more than mere research. There was something about her energy signature that resonated with his own in a way he hadn't anticipated. And tonight, he would observe her performance, perhaps even attempt the private lesson she had mentioned.

For mission objectives, of course. Nothing more.

Behind him, Eclipse and Lunar had moved to their respective areas of the suite, each claiming their territory as naturally as they would have on Zorveya.

Some patterns, it seemed, were universal.

5

By nine o'clock, The Crash Zone was packed. Friday night after a UFO sighting was prime time for Duskrock's particular brand of tourism. The bar hummed with excited chatter, the ceiling's half-hearted alien decorations, metallic streamers, and hanging cardboard flying saucers catching the colored lights as they swept across the room.

Dani sat in the small back room that served as both storage and her preparation space, applying the final touches to her makeup. For performances, she painted her face with swirls of red and gold that caught the firelight and enhanced her expressions. It was part of the persona. Dani Ember. Fire dancer. Untouchable and mesmerizing.

Different from Danielle Evans, the girl who'd

run away from foster care at sixteen. Different from the Dani who'd bounced between cities and jobs, always looking for somewhere that felt like belonging.

"Fifteen minutes," Mike called through the door. "We've got a line out front."

"I'll be ready," she replied, smudging the gold paint along her cheekbone.

Her fire tools were prepped, wicks freshly trimmed, and ready for fuel. The poi, weighted balls at the end of chains that she would spin in mesmerizing patterns of flame, sat beside her fire fans and staff. Each tool had its own personality, its own rhythm in her hands. Tonight, she'd use all of them.

The crowd would be entertained. She desperately needed the tips.

A knock at the door interrupted her thoughts. "Someone asking for you," Mike said, poking his head in. "Golden boy. Got a weird name. Says you invited him."

Dani's heart skipped. "Solar?"

"That's the one. Want me to send him back?"

She hesitated, checking the time. "No. Tell him I'll see him after the show. He can have the table near the stage."

Mike raised an eyebrow but didn't comment.

"You got it, firegirl. I'll tell you mystery date no pre-show nookie."

"Don't say nookie. You're a grown man."

"Ten minutes."

When he left, Dani stared at her reflection, unsure why her pulse had quickened. Solar was just another guy. Probably just another passing interest. Duskrock was full of travelers, people who came and went with the seasonal shifts in tourism.

And yet there had been something in his eyes. Something ancient and knowing that didn't match his awkward words. A tremor of anticipation worked through her.

"Stop being horny. Focus," she told her reflection. "The fire demands it."

She pushed thoughts of Solar aside and began her final preparations, rolling her shoulders and neck to release tension. Fire had no patience for distraction. Every movement had to be precise, deliberate. One mistake could mean burns or worse.

When Mike's voice boomed over the sound system announcing her, Dani was ready. She stepped out into the main room, walked purposefully to the center of her performance space, and took a deep breath.

The crowd fell silent. The lights dimmed. And

there, at the table closest to the stage, sat Solar. He wasn't watching her. Instead, he stared transfixed at the unlit fire poi in her hands.

Dani smiled. Time to show him what real fire manipulation looked like.

Her background music started to play. With practiced motions, she dipped the wicks in fuel, shook off the excess, and struck a match. The first touch of flame to wick was always magical, that initial flare, the gentle whoosh as fire came to life in her hands.

The crowd gasped appreciatively, but Dani wasn't performing for them. For the first time in years, she found herself performing for an audience of one.

Solar's eyes widened as the flames caught and grew, his face illuminated in the firelight. And as Dani began to move, spinning the poi in ever more complex patterns, she saw something in his expression shift from curiosity to recognition.

In that moment, with fire dancing between them, Dani felt a strange certainty.

This man understood fire in a way no one else in her life ever had.

The music pulsed through the bar as Dani transitioned from poi to fire fans, the flames creating sweeping arcs of light. Each movement was precisely choreographed, perfected through years of practice. The heat caressed her skin, a familiar companion, as she manipulated the fire with the confidence of someone who had tamed a wild thing.

But tonight felt different. The flames seemed more responsive, more alive. She risked a glance at Solar between movements. His attention never wavered. He leaned forward, elbows on the table, golden eyes reflecting the fire with an intensity that made her skin tingle. Was it her imagination, or was his skin actually glowing beneath his loose-fitting shirt?

As she moved into the most challenging part of her routine, Dani felt a surge of adrenaline. She wanted to impress him. Reaching for her fire staff, she spun it between her hands, creating a whirlwind of flame that drew appreciative murmurs from the crowd.

"For my final act," she announced, raising her voice to carry over the music, "I'll need complete darkness."

Solar's expression became tense, and he sat back in his chair.

The bar lights dimmed further until only her flames illuminated the space. Dani had performed this finale dozens of times, a complex sequence that involved extinguishing and relighting the staff in a precise pattern that created the illusion of floating fire.

She began the sequence, spinning the staff faster. The crowd's faces blurred into darkness beyond the circle of firelight. Only Solar remained distinct, his features sharpened by the contrast of light and shadow. The firelight liked him, causing him to glow brighter than the rest of the crowd. Or maybe he simply had her focus.

Then, as she executed a particularly difficult maneuver, Dani felt something change. The fire surged, growing hotter, brighter. The flames stretched unnaturally long, as if reaching for something.

Reaching for Solar.

Startled, she missed her timing. The staff wobbled in her hands. One end dipped too low, catching the edge of her costume sleeve. Fire raced up the fabric with hungry intensity.

The crowd gasped, this time in alarm. Dani dropped the staff and tried to smother the flames, but they spread with unnatural speed.

Suddenly, Solar was there, moving impossibly fast. He caught her arm, and instead of smothering the flames, he did something strange. His bare hand passed through the fire, and rather than burning him, the flames seemed to flow into his skin, absorbed like water into sand.

In seconds, the fire was gone, leaving only warm fabric and a strange, electric tingling where his fingers gripped her arm.

The bar erupted in applause, assuming it was part of the act. But Dani stared at Solar, speechless, as the house lights came up.

Mike appeared next to the performance area with a fire extinguisher.

The sound of the crowd forced her into an automatic bow. Several were coming forward to put money in the tip jar Mike kept for the entertainers.

"Thank you!" Dani gave a wave before grabbing Solar's wrist. She pulled him toward the back hallway, away from the curious eyes of the crowd.

Mike followed them, scanning her for injuries. "What happened? Are you okay?"

"I'm fine," Dani assured him, not taking her eyes off Solar.

"That was some quick thinking, buddy," Mike said to Solar, clapping him on the shoulder. "Those flames went out like magic."

"Fire responds to my energy signature," Solar answered seriously.

Mike arched a brow and looked as if he wasn't sure if he should laugh or not.

"Basic fire safety. Nothing unusual," Dani explained. She forced a nervous laugh. "I told you tonight's act was going to be on fire."

Mike looked between them, sensing the tension. "Right. Well, great set, Dani. I'll have Jessie bring you both drinks, on the house."

"That wasn't basic fire safety," she said once they were alone. "I've been working with fire for fifteen years. My clothes are flame-retardant. They should not have lit on fire like that. But I know what I saw. It wasn't natural. How did you—?"

"You were in danger," he said simply, his voice low. Solar's expression remained neutral, but his skin had a subtle glow that seemed to pulse beneath the surface. "Your demonstration was impressive. The manipulation techniques could be useful for—"

"Don't change the subject." Dani stepped closer, studying his face. This close, she could feel heat radiating from him, like standing near a furnace. "What are you? You're not..."

She almost said he wasn't human, but the word

stuck in her throat. If he wasn't human, what did that leave? Supernatural? Extraterrestrial?

For a moment, he seemed to consider lying. Then something shifted in his expression. "You understand fire. You respect its power, its patterns. Perhaps you can understand me as well."

He held out his hand, palm up, and before her eyes, a small flame appeared, hovering just above his skin without burning him. It danced and swirled, responding to the subtle movements of his fingers.

"I am of the Solarus Zone," he said quietly. "My people evolved in perpetual daylight, absorbing and channeling solar energy as naturally as you breathe."

Dani should have been terrified, or at least skeptical. Instead, she felt a rush of exhilaration. "You're from the ship that crashed yesterday. That wasn't another hoax?"

Solar nodded. "I am one of three representatives sent to your planet on a diplomatic mission."

"Diplomatic," Dani repeated, raising an eyebrow. "And that mission involves watching fire dancers in sketchy bars?"

A hint of a smile touched his lips. "It involves finding compatible Earth females who might help demonstrate that cooperation between different species is possible."

"Compatible Earth females," Dani echoed, a warmth spreading through her that had nothing to do with the lingering heat of her performance. "And am I compatible?"

Solar's glow intensified slightly. "Your energy signature resonates with mine in ways I did not anticipate. It is why the flames responded to you so strongly." He extinguished the fire in his palm with a subtle closing of his fist. "They recognized something familiar."

Before Dani could respond, a waitress appeared with two drinks. "Mike said to give you these. Great show tonight, Dani! That finale was wild."

"Thanks, Jessie," Dani replied automatically, taking the drinks.

When they were alone again, she handed one to Solar. "So, what happens now? Do you abduct me to your spaceship for experiments?"

Solar looked genuinely offended. "I am a warrior of the Solarus Elite Guard, not a primitive specimen collector. If any association forms between us, it would be voluntary and mutual."

"Association," Dani repeated, taking a sip of her drink. The alcohol burned pleasantly down her throat. "Is that what they call it on your planet?"

Solar's confusion was evident. "Call what?"

Dani laughed, the tension breaking. "Never mind. Look, I need to change and collect my tips. Why don't you wait for me? We can go somewhere quieter to talk about this energy signature compatibility thing."

Solar nodded, his formal demeanor softening. "I would find that acceptable."

"Acceptable," she mimicked with a smile. "You really know how to make a girl feel special."

He nodded in agreement. "Yes."

"And you're modest, too," she laughed.

She slipped into the back room, her heart racing as she quickly changed and removed her performance makeup. An alien. She was flirting with an actual alien who could manipulate fire. Even by Duskrock standards, this was bizarre.

Well, she was always attracted to the flame.

She couldn't remember the last time she'd felt so alive. The way he'd watched her perform awakened something in her.

When she emerged, Solar was waiting precisely where she'd left him, standing with perfect stillness. His eyes tracked her movement, and that subtle glow beneath his skin seemed to brighten at her approach.

"Ready?" she asked, suddenly nervous.

"Yes," he answered simply. "Where shall we go?"

Dani considered for a moment. "My place is close. We can walk."

The desert night was cool, stars brilliant in the clear sky. They walked in silence for several blocks, Dani acutely aware of the heat radiating from Solar's body beside her. He moved with a grace that reminded her of flames dancing in still air.

"I do not like this darkness, but you make it tolerable. Your world has many stars," Solar observed as they walked. "On Zorveya, my zone sees only eternal day. The stars are known to most only through education, not experience. Very few of us venture into the twilight zone."

Dani tried to suppress a laugh.

"Is something amusing about that?"

"Twilight zone?" She nodded and laughed harder. "I mean, yeah. I think I might be in the twilight zone right now."

He looked up. "No. I do not think so. I believe you call this unwelcoming time the night."

"Twilight Zone is an old television show where strange things happen to," she paused, "you know what, never mind. It's not important.'

"Ah, yes, your television. We were shown your depictions of aliens on our journey here." He frowned. "They were not completely accurate."

"So, always sunlight, you said? That sounds beautiful and terrible at the same time," Dani changed the subject. "Never seeing stars, but also never knowing darkness."

Solar glanced at her. "You, a person of the fire, enjoy this dark sky?"

"Yes, I prefer the balance of light and dark. I think you need both to appreciate either," she said, surprising herself with the philosophical turn. "Fire means nothing without shadow to define it."

Solar seemed to consider this. "Perhaps that is why the council sent representatives from both zones, with Eclipse to mediate between us."

"Eclipse? That's your friend from the twilight zone?"

"The correct Earth translation for his land is called the Twilight Belt," Solar corrected. "Yes. He maintains balance between those of light and shadow."

They reached her small apartment, a second-floor unit in an adobe complex with a view of the red rocks. Dani fumbled with her keys, suddenly self-conscious about the modest space.

"It's not much," she said, opening the door. "But it's home for now."

Solar entered, his eyes taking in every detail with

careful assessment. "You have many fire implements," he noted, gesturing to the practice tools hanging on her wall and propped up in a corner.

"It's more than a job," Dani admitted, setting down her bag. "It's the only thing that ever made sense to me. The only time I feel fully in control."

Solar moved to the window, looking out at the night sky. "Control is an illusion. Fire knows this. It can be directed but never truly contained."

Dani stepped closer to him, drawn by the warmth of his presence. "Is that what you are? Fire that can't be contained?"

Solar turned to face her, his golden eyes reflecting the dim light of her apartment. "My people believe in harnessing energy, focusing it to achieve our goals. But yes, there is always a risk of burning too bright."

"And what's your goal here, on Earth?" Dani asked, her voice dropping to a near whisper. She studied his skin. It looked like some kind of shell meant to hide who he really was beneath.

"Officially? To demonstrate that cooperation between different beings is possible." His gaze intensified. "But I find myself developing unauthorized objectives."

Dani smiled, closing the distance between them.

Her adrenaline from being set on fire was still surging in her veins. She couldn't help but think she was a moth to his flame. She needed to get closer to him. "Such as?"

"Understanding why your fire manipulation techniques affect my energy patterns," he said, but his voice had roughened. "And why I cannot stop thinking about the way your body moves when you dance."

The directness of his statement sent heat coursing through her. "Maybe we should investigate that. For science."

"For science," Solar agreed, his lips curving in what might have been his first genuine smile.

Thank goodness this alien man got flirting.

Dani reached up, hesitantly touching his face. His skin was hot beneath her fingers, not uncomfortably so, but warmer than any human's should be. The subtle glow intensified where she made contact.

She wondered if their bodies would be compatible. Every nerve in her begged her to find out. Her eyes dipped down his body. He looked human, or in the very least, *humanoid*. There seemed to be a bulge between his thighs that gave her growing desire hope. She couldn't help but think of how good his heat would feel inside her.

Her heartbeat quickened, and she naturally leaned closer, wondering at the shape of him beneath the fake skin.

"I want to see the real you," she whispered, surprising herself with the admission.

Solar's hand covered hers, pressing her palm more firmly against his cheek. "You control fire as if you were born to it. On my world, such skill would mark you as elite."

The compliment, so specific to her unique talent, touched something deep within her. Dani had never felt particularly special or valued. Fire had been her only constant companion, the only thing that didn't leave or disappoint her.

Until now, perhaps.

"I have seen this on your television." When Solar leaned down to kiss her, it felt inevitable. His lips were surprisingly soft, but that same heat radiated from them, sending sparks of pleasure racing across her skin. Dani pressed closer, her hands moving to his shoulders, feeling the strange, smooth texture of the skin beneath his shirt.

The kiss deepened, and Solar's initial hesitancy gave way to a hunger that matched her own. His hands found her waist, pulling her against him with careful strength that suggested he was holding back.

Her heart beat fast and hard. She wanted to explore the danger churning inside him.

"It's okay," she murmured against his mouth. "I'm not fragile."

Something seemed to break loose in him at her words. His arms tightened around her, and the temperature between them rose noticeably. The kiss became more demanding, his tongue meeting hers with a skill that suggested some aspects of attraction were definitely universal.

Dani's fingers found the buttons of his shirt, working them free with growing urgency. She needed to see more of him, to understand what lay beneath the human disguise.

As the shirt fell open, she gasped. The skin armor of his chest was perfectly sculpted, muscular, and smooth, but it was the shimmering gold luminescence that pulsed through the barrier like a heartbeat that held her gaze. Intricate patterns, like muted solar flares, moved beneath the surface.

"You're magnificent," she breathed, trailing her fingers over the living light of his torso.

Solar shuddered at her touch. "The skin-suit is failing," he said, his voice strained. "Your proximity accelerates the deterioration."

"Then take it off," Dani suggested, boldness over-coming caution. "I want to see the real you."

Uncertainty flickered across his face. "My true form is intense. The light may be too much for your human perception."

"I work with fire," Dani reminded him, stepping back to pull her own shirt over her head. "I'm not afraid of a little brightness."

Solar's eyes widened at the sight of her bare body, the movement of the light beneath his skin quicken-ing. With deliberate care, he removed his shirt completely, then reached for something at the back of his neck. There was a soft hissing sound, and the skin-suit began to peel off like a membrane.

As it fell away, pure golden light filled the room. Solar stood before her, his true form revealed, a being made of contained sunlight. The patterns she had glimpsed beneath his skin now danced freely across his surface, solar flares and cosmic fire swirling in mesmerizing patterns.

Dani's breath caught. She had expected some-thing alien, but not this living art, this embodiment of fire and light. His body maintained a humanoid shape, perfectly proportioned and masculine, but composed entirely of golden energy that pulsed and flowed like liquid flame.

"You're not afraid," Solar observed, his voice deeper now, resonating with power that made the air vibrate around them.

"Should I be?" Dani asked, unable to look away.

"Most species find our true form overwhelming." His light dimmed slightly, as if he were consciously restraining himself. "It can be dangerous to touch."

Dani smiled and stepped closer, the heat from his body washing over her skin. "I've been playing with fire my whole life. Danger and I are old friends."

Reaching out, she placed her palm against his chest. The sensation was unlike anything she'd ever experienced, warm but not burning, solid yet flowing, like touching the heart of a candle flame that somehow held form. Energy tingled up her arm, spreading through her body with a pleasure so intense it bordered on pain.

Solar trembled beneath her touch. "Your body conducts my energy," he said, wonder in his voice. "This is unexpected."

"Good unexpected?" Dani asked, trailing her fingers across the living light of his torso.

In answer, Solar caught her hand and brought it to his lips, kissing her palm with careful restraint. The touch sent a jolt of heat straight to her core. "Very good," he murmured against her skin.

His hand moved to cup her face, fingers tracing the line of her jaw with reverence. The sensation was incredible, each touch sending ripples of pleasure through her nervous system. Dani leaned into his palm, wanting more.

"I have studied Earth mating customs," Solar said, his reserved tone at odds with the intimate moment. "But I find myself uncertain of proper protocol. Your species has many complex rituals."

Dani couldn't help but laugh. "Protocol?" She reached behind her back, unclasping her bra and letting it fall away. "How's this for protocol?"

Solar's glow intensified, the light in the room brightening in response to his reaction. His eyes, now pure golden fire, traveled over her exposed skin with undisguised hunger.

"Very efficient," he managed, his voice strained.

Dani took his hands and guided them to her breasts. The contact was electric, his energy pouring wildly into her, heightening every sensation. She gasped as pleasure coursed through her body, more intense than anything she'd ever felt with a human lover.

Solar watched her reactions with fascination, learning quickly what made her breath catch, what drew soft sounds from her throat. He was a fast study, adjusting pressure and movement based on her responses.

"You are exquisite," he murmured, bending to replace his hands with his mouth.

Dani cried out at the first touch of his lips on her breast. The heat was extraordinary, pleasure spiraling through her body in waves. She tangled her fingers in the light where his hair would be, surprised to find it had substance, like touching warm silk that moved against her skin.

"Bedroom," she managed between gasps. "Down the hall."

Solar lifted her with effortless strength, cradling her against his glowing form. The entire length of his body radiated heat against hers, and tiny particles began to lift from his skin as if he floated freely. He drifted with her into the darkness of her bedroom. In the unlit room, he was the only source of illumination, casting golden light across her simple furnishings.

His body regained its form and he laid her on the bed with surprising gentleness, standing back to look at her with an expression of wonder. Dani took the opportunity to remove her remaining clothes, the cool air a stark contrast to the heat emanating from Solar's form.

"You're still wearing too much," she said, nodding to the lower portion of the pants and skin-suit that clung to his hips and legs.

Solar hesitated. "Full exposure may be overwhelming."

"I'll take my chances."

With a fluid motion, Solar removed his pants. The bulge she'd noticed hung like a dead weight between his thighs as part of the suit, not part of his true form. He then took off the rest of the membrane. He became fully revealed, masculine and powerful, and his energy concentrated and intensified in ways that left no doubt about his desire for her.

Dani's eyes widened. The flat energy between his legs began to reshape, mimicking that of a well-endowed human male.

Solar moved onto the bed beside her, careful not to press his full weight against her. "Your body temperature is elevated," he observed, trailing a finger down her throat to the valley between her breasts. "Your pulse is rapid. These are signs of arousal in humans, correct?"

"Very correct," Dani breathed. "And what are the signs of arousal for your species?"

Solar's light pulsed visibly, brightening and dimming in a rhythm she found hypnotic. "Increased energy output. Heightened thermal radiation. Disruption of normal light patterns." His voice deepened further. "All of which I am experiencing at dangerous levels."

"Dangerous how?" she asked, running her hands over his shoulders, reveling in the strange texture of his skin, like touching living electricity.

"I could burn you," he admitted. "If I lose control."

Dani smiled up at him. "Then don't lose control. I trust you."

Something shifted in his expression at her words. Trust. Such a simple human concept, yet it seemed to affect him.

His kiss was careful at first, measured, but as Dani responded with increasing passion, his restraint began to slip. The temperature between them rose, his light brightening until the entire room was bathed in golden radiance.

His hands explored her body with growing confidence, learning the terrain of her curves and hollows. When his fingers finally slipped between her thighs, finding her wet and ready, the energy that flowed from his touch sent her arching off the bed with a cry of shocked pleasure.

"Did I hurt you?" Solar asked immediately, withdrawing his hand.

"Hell, no," Dani gasped. "Please don't stop."

He continued his exploration, watching her reactions with intense focus. Each touch sent pulses of energy through her nervous system, building pleasure in ways she'd never experienced. It was as if he could direct sensation itself, concentrating it where she needed it most.

When she was trembling on the edge, desperate and begging for completion, she guided him over her. "I want you," she whispered. "All of you."

Solar positioned himself between her thighs, his expression a mixture of desire and concern. "I will try to maintain control."

His energy flowed into her rather than thrust, expanding to fill her to the brink. The press of his body drew a gasp from them both. His energy flowed into her as their bodies joined. Tiny sparks exploded over his skin like fireworks. They rained down on her, tingling wherever they met flesh. His body dissolved into pure energy, barely keeping shape.

"You pull at my essence," he said, his voice filled with wonder. "This is not painful for you?"

"It's incredible," Dani assured him, wrapping her legs around his waist to draw him deeper. Her legs sank into his energy field before finding a solid core to hold on to. Everything pulsed and tingled.

Solar began to ripple within her, each undulating wave of sexual energy sending heat and pleasure through her body. The room grew brighter still, his control slipping as passion overtook his restraint. Where their skin met, Dani glowed with a sympathetic light, as if his energy was flowing through her, being absorbed and reflected back.

The sensation built. Dani clung to him, writhing with growing urgency. Solar's throbbing rhythm quickened, his light pulsing in time with their shared passion.

When release finally claimed her, it was like being consumed by fire from the inside out. Pleasure exploded through every nerve, the current arching her body as wave after wave of sensation moved through her. Moments later, Solar's control broke, and his light flared with blinding intensity. She had to close her eyes and turn her head.

When Dani opened her eyes, she saw through him to the cosmic energy at his core. Every piece of her hummed. The connection was so profound that it transcended the physical. Then the light receded, leaving them tangled together in the dimness of her bedroom, skin against skin, human and alien joined in the aftermath of passion.

Solar's weight pressed her into the mattress, but

Dani didn't mind. His body still radiated heat, like lying next to a fire pit. She traced patterns on his back, following the swirls of light that moved beneath his surface.

"Did I harm you?" he asked finally, lifting himself slightly to study her face in the golden glow he still emitted.

Dani stretched, cataloging the pleasant ache in her muscles, the lingering warmth that suffused her entire body. "No. You didn't hurt me."

"Your skin," Solar touched her shoulder gently. "It's marked."

Dani glanced down to see faint patterns on her skin, like luminous temporary tattoos where his hands had gripped her most tightly. They didn't hurt, and even as she watched, they began to fade.

"Battle scars," she joked. "I'll survive."

Solar rolled onto his side, bringing her with him so they faced each other on the pillow. His expression was thoughtful, almost confused. "This was not part of the mission parameters."

Dani couldn't help but laugh. "Is that your way of saying this was a one-night stand?"

"I do not understand that term."

"It means sex without commitment. Just physical, nothing more." Dani tried to keep her tone light, though something in her chest tightened at the thought.

Solar's brow furrowed. "Is that what you desire? A temporary physical connection?"

Dani hesitated. What did she want? This was literally an alien from another planet. There was no future here, no possibility of anything lasting.

And yet...

"I don't know," she admitted. "This isn't exactly covered in the dating handbook."

Solar's hand moved to her face, cupping her cheek with surprising tenderness. "On Zorveya, energy compatibility is rare and valued. What we experienced, the way your body conducts and harmonizes with my essence, is not something I would discard lightly."

Hope flickered in Dani's chest, small but persistent. "So, what are you saying?"

"I am saying that while temporary physical connection was not my intention, neither was finding someone whose energy signature resonates with mine in ways I never anticipated." His thumb traced the curve of her lower lip. "I would like to explore this further. If that is acceptable to you."

Dani smiled, warmth spreading through her that had nothing to do with his alien heat. "Yeah, that's acceptable." She pressed a kiss to his palm. "Very acceptable."

Solar's golden eyes softened, his light dimming to a gentle glow that bathed them both in warmth. Outside, the desert night continued, stars wheeling across the sky above a world where fire dancers could find unexpected connections with beings made of light and heat, where the impossible suddenly seemed within reach.

6

SOLAR EMERGED FROM TRYING TO RECHARGE HIS energy during the human sleep cycle hours to unfamiliar sensations. The first was softness beneath him, different from the rigid sleeping platforms of Zorveya or even the inadequate bed at Crimson Rock Inn. The second was warmth pressed against his side, a source of heat separate from his own energy. The third, most disorienting, was darkness.

He opened his eyes to find himself in Dani's apartment, morning light filtering through partially closed blinds, creating stripes of gold across the tangled bedding. Beside him, Dani slept, her red hair spread across the pillow like flame frozen in time, her breathing deep and even. It wasn't lost on him that he'd been critical of Lunar and Eclipse for revealing their natures so readily to Earth females, and here he was entangled with one.

Solar studied her with scientific curiosity. The concept of unconsciousness as a regular biological function was foreign to his kind. In the eternal daylight of the Solarus Zone, rest happened in brief intervals of reduced activity while maintaining awareness. This human vulnerability, this complete surrender to unconsciousness, seemed both inefficient and strangely compelling.

His skin had returned to its contained state overnight, the golden light dimmed to a subtle glow rather than the full radiance he had released during their coupling. The deteriorated skin-suit lay discarded on the floor, useless now that its integrity had been compromised. He would need to conceal his true nature through other means until Galaxy Brides provided replacements, assuming the incompetent corporation ever managed to deliver on their promises.

Dani stirred beside him, her body shifting as consciousness gradually returned. Solar found the process fascinating, watching as awareness slowly reclaimed her features. Her eyes opened, focusing on him with momentary confusion before recognition and memory settled in her expression.

"You're still here," she murmured, her voice rough with sleep.

"Yes," Solar confirmed. "Where else would I be?"

A smile curved her lips. "I don't know. Flying back to your planet? Reporting to your alien bosses? Making crop circles?"

"I have no agricultural duties," Solar informed her. "And communication with Zorveya is currently impossible without proper equipment."

Dani laughed, the sound warming something inside him that had nothing to do with his natural energy regulation. "It was a joke. Humans often fear that after sex, the other person will run out in the middle of the night."

"That would be impractical," Solar pointed out. "How would we have sex again if I left? Besides, my assigned dwelling is several kilometers from this location, and I have no transportation device or working skin-suit."

"Yes, you're very practical," Dani said, stretching beside him. The movement drew his attention to the curves of her body, partially revealed by the sheets. His energy output increased automatically in response, creating a subtle brightening of his skin.

Dani noticed the change, her eyes widening slightly. "You're glowing again."

"Your proximity affects my energy containment," Solar admitted. "The reaction is involuntary."

"So I literally turn you on?" She grinned, clearly pleased by the concept.

Solar considered this. "If by turn on you mean you activate increased energy output, then yes. Your biorhythms create resonance patterns that stimulate my natural emissions."

"That might be the weirdest and hottest compliment I've ever gotten." Dani sat up, letting the sheet fall away, unconcerned by her nakedness. "I need coffee. Do aliens drink coffee?"

"I have not attempted this substance," Solar replied. "I have seen many humans obsessively consuming it, but it has a questionable smell."

"That's because, for some humans, coffee is life." Dani slipped from the bed, pulling on a loose shirt that fell to mid-thigh.

Solar watched her move around the small kitchen area, appreciating the efficiency of her movements. Unlike many humans he had observed since arrival, Dani wasted no motion. Each action flowed into the next with precision that reminded him of combat training exercises.

"You move like a warrior," he observed.

Dani glanced back at him, eyebrows raised.

"That's a new one. Usually guys tell me I move like a dancer."

"There is similarity," Solar acknowledged. "Both require discipline and body control. But you have economy of motion that suggests training beyond performance."

The coffee machine gurgled, releasing an aroma that Solar found strange. His olfactory analysis identified complex compounds, many with potential energy properties.

"I've trained in various martial arts since I was twelve," Dani admitted, leaning against the counter as she waited for the coffee to brew. "Started with basic self-defense classes at the community center. The foster family I was with thought it might help with my anger issues."

"You were separated from your biological family unit?" Solar asked, recalling information from their Earth cultural briefing about human child-rearing practices.

"My parents died when I was eight. Car accident." Dani's voice remained matter-of-fact, though Solar detected subtle changes in her energy pattern that suggested emotional undercurrents. "I bounced around the foster system until I ran away at sixteen."

Solar processed this information against what he

knew of Earth's social structures. "You were assigned to surrogate caretakers who proved inadequate."

"Some weren't bad," Dani said with a small shrug. "But none of them were family. By sixteen, I'd figured out I was better off taking care of myself."

The coffee finished brewing, and Dani poured two mugs, adding a white powder to one before bringing them both to the bed. She offered the modified beverage to Solar.

"I added sugar to yours. Might help with the bitterness if you're not used to it."

Solar accepted the mug, analyzing the steaming liquid with his enhanced senses. The temperature was low but within his tolerance, and the chemical composition suggested potential energy conversion properties. He took a careful sip, allowing his system to process the new substance.

It smelled better than it tasted.

"This contains stimulants," he noted after a moment. "Compounds that affect neural function."

"That's the point," Dani confirmed, settling cross-legged on the bed facing him, her own mug cradled in both hands. "Helps humans wake up and function."

Solar set the cup down. "It is not agreeable to my mouth."

"Try mine." She offered her mug.

He braced himself, but obliged her by taking a sip. The taste was much better. "Yes. This one is acceptable."

"Alien man likes his coffee black," Dani said as she went back to the kitchen. She returned with a new mug.

Solar took another sip. His body was already converting the compounds into useful energy, though the process was inefficient compared to direct solar absorption.

"You have adapted to self-sufficiency at an early age," he observed, returning to their previous conversation. "This demonstrates notable survival capability."

Dani's expression softened slightly. "Most people say it's sad, not impressive."

"Survival is always impressive," Solar stated definitively. "On Zorveya, independence is valued, particularly in the Solarus Zone where resource competition can be intense."

"What about family?" Dani asked. "Don't your people care about that?"

"Family units are important for initial development and resource allocation," Solar explained. "But ultimate loyalty belongs to the zone. I have siblings whom I help to resource, but our connections are formalized through zone hierarchy rather than emotional bonds."

Dani considered this, sipping her coffee. "Sounds lonely."

The concept gave Solar pause. Loneliness was not a state recognized in Solarus culture. Isolation, yes, as a tactical disadvantage. But the emotional component Dani implied was unfamiliar.

"It is efficient," he said finally. "Emotional attachments complicate tactical decision-making."

"So says the alien who's having breakfast in bed with a human woman after a night of mind-blowing sex," Dani pointed out with a small smile.

Solar couldn't argue with the factual accuracy of her statement. His presence here directly contradicted standard Solarus protocols regarding mission parameters and interpersonal engagement. Yet he found himself unwilling to correct the discrepancy.

"My behavior has become inconsistent with standard operating procedures," he acknowledged. "Your energy signature creates exceptions."

Dani's smile widened. "I'm your exception?"

Before Solar could respond, a sharp electronic tone sounded from somewhere in the tangled bedding. Dani frowned, setting down her coffee to search for the source.

"That's not my phone," she muttered, finally locating a small device partially hidden beneath a pillow. "Is this yours?"

Solar recognized the communication unit Gary had given him before abandoning them on Earth. The device had been silent since their arrival, its sudden activation potentially significant.

"Yes," he confirmed, taking it from her. "It must have fallen off my head."

The screen displayed an unfamiliar symbol, pulsing in a pattern that indicated urgent contact. Solar pressed his thumb against the recognition pad, activating the secure communication protocol.

A holographic projection emerged from the device, flickering before stabilizing to display Gary's yellow face. The image was distorted, suggesting transmission difficulties.

"Solar. Thank the cosmic constants," Gary's voice crackled with static. "We've been trying to reach you for hours."

"You abandoned us on this planet with minimal resources and inadequate skin-suits," Solar reminded him, his tone hardening. "Your concern seems belated."

"Yes, well, about that," Gary shifted uncomfortably. "There have been complications. The ship required more extensive repairs than anticipated, and then there was an unfortunate incident occurred with local wildlife. Did you know Earth has creatures called mountain lions that are neither mountains nor lions? Quite aggressive. They chewed on Harris."

"State your purpose," Solar demanded, his patience for the alien's rambling explanations exhausted.

Gary's expression turned serious, the change notable even through the distorted projection. "You're being tracked. All three of you. We've detected multiple Earth scanning technologies focusing on the crash site and spreading outward. Someone knows you're there and is actively searching."

Solar's combat instincts immediately activated, his skin brightening with battle-readiness. Beside him, Dani watched with wide eyes, clearly able to see and hear the holographic communication. His inept tour guide's translator spoke in her native language.

"What kind of tracking technology?" Solar asked, already calculating defensive options.

"Satellite surveillance, electromagnetic sensors, ground-based teams with specialized equipment," Gary listed. "Far beyond typical Earth capabilities.

We believe it's an organization called Milano Enterprises. We have had dealings with them in the past. We sent their leader on a one-way trip to... well, never mind where, but it seems his corporation lives on without him. These human collectives are hard beasts to kill without breaking several intergalactic treaties."

Dani made a small sound of recognition. Solar glanced at her, noting her suddenly heightened attention.

"The Milano *Foundation?*" she asked, leaning closer to the projection. "The charity people? They're looking for them?"

Gary's hologram turned toward her, eyes blinking rapidly. "Ah, I see you've found a human mate! Excellent progress on the mission objectives. And yes, Milano Enterprises and their foundation arm appear to be coordinating the search efforts. They have resources and knowledge that suggest multiple previous extraterrestrial contacts."

"Previous contacts?" Solar demanded. "Your briefing materials indicated Earth had no official awareness of alien life."

"Official awareness, no," Gary hedged. "But there have been, shall we say, incidents over the years. The Killian situation wasn't the first, merely the most recent. Milano may have acquired technology or knowledge from previous crashes."

"We are compromised," Solar concluded, his tactical assessment grim. "Our cover identities will not withstand targeted investigation."

"Precisely why I'm contacting you," Gary agreed. "We've accelerated our timeline. Extraction in forty-eight Earth hours. You need to gather Eclipse and Lunar and proceed to these coordinates." A series of numbers appeared beside Gary's projection. "We'll have replacement supplies and transportation waiting."

"Forty-eight hours?" Solar repeated. "Your previous estimate was thirty Earth days."

"Yes, well, circumstances change," Gary said vaguely. "The Milano situation creates unacceptable risk levels. The council would be most displeased if Earth authorities captured their representatives."

"Or perhaps the council would find it convenient if we simply disappeared," Solar suggested, his suspicion of the mission's true purpose resurging. "Permanent exile through convenient accident."

Gary's hologram flickered, whether from transmission issues or discomfort with the accusation was unclear. "I'm sure I don't know what you mean.

Galaxy Alien Mail Order Brides provides quality service with guaranteed satisfaction."

"Your guarantees have proven worthless," Solar stated flatly.

"Nevertheless, the extraction will proceed as scheduled," Gary insisted. "Forty-eight hours, Solar. Be there with the others, or risk permanent stranding on Earth." With that, the hologram flickered and disappeared.

Solar stared at the now-inactive device, his mind racing with tactical assessments and contingency plans. The communication had confirmed his suspicions about the mission while introducing new variables that required immediate action.

"So," Dani's voice broke into his thoughts. "When were you going to mention that the Milano Foundation is hunting aliens?"

Solar turned to find her watching him intently, her expression a complex mixture of concern and something that might have been hurt.

"I was unaware of their involvement until now," he answered truthfully. "Our briefing materials indicated minimal risk of Earth authorities detecting our presence."

"The Milano Foundation isn't just any Earth authority," Dani said. "They're a major corporation with government contracts. If they're looking for you, it's serious."

"You have prior knowledge of this organization," Solar observed.

Dani nodded, her expression darkening. "They run lots of charities. They sponsor fire safety programs in schools. I've done performances at their events. But there have always been rumors about their research division. Strange experiments, unexplained phenomena around their test sites. Most people think it's conspiracy theory nonsense."

"It appears the conspiracy theories contain elements of truth," Solar noted. "If they have encountered alien technology before, they may have capabilities beyond typical Earth science."

"And now they're looking for you." Dani's voice held an edge of concern that Solar found unexpectedly affecting. "What are you going to do?"

Solar considered his options. The mission parameters had changed significantly. Extraction in forty-eight hours meant abandoning the diplomatic experiment that had brought them to Earth. It also meant leaving Dani.

The thought created an unexpected disruption in his energy flow, a discordant pattern that suggested emotional involvement beyond his conscious intent.

Solar found himself reluctant to accept the necessity of separation.

"I must contact Eclipse and Lunar," he said finally. "We must coordinate our response to this new information."

"And then what?" Dani pressed. "You just leave? Zip back to your planet like none of this happened?"

The question contained layers Solar wasn't equipped to fully process. His training as a Solarus Elite Guard emphasized mission objectives over personal connections. Yet his experience with Dani had created something that defied standard classification.

"I don't know," he admitted, the uncertainty itself a novel experience. Warriors of the Solarus Zone did not acknowledge doubt or indecision. "The mission parameters have altered beyond my pre-established response protocols."

Dani studied him for a moment, then set her mug aside with deliberate care. "Okay, let me make this simpler. Do you want to leave?"

The directness of the question cut through Solar's calculations, forcing him to confront the core issue. Did he want to leave Earth? Leave Dani?

"No," he answered, surprising himself with the immediacy and certainty of his response. "Your energy signature creates resonance patterns unlike any I have encountered. The connection between us is significant. I do not wish to sever it."

A smile slowly spread across Dani's face. "That might be the most romantic thing an alien warrior has ever said to me."

"It is factually accurate," Solar insisted, though he recognized her attempt at humor.

"So if you don't want to go, don't go," Dani said simply. "Stay here. With me."

"Remaining would mean abandoning my responsibilities to the Solarus Zone," Solar pointed out, though the argument felt hollow even as he made it. "And potentially stranding myself on Earth permanently."

"Would that be so terrible?" Dani asked softly. "Earth has sunlight. And fire dancers. And coffee."

The offer was tempting in ways Solar had not anticipated when beginning this mission. Earth, for all its primitive technology and chaotic social structures, offered freedoms unknown on Zorveya. Here, he wasn't merely a component of the Solarus military apparatus. Here, with Dani, he was simply Solar, valued for his individual energy signature rather than his tactical utility.

"I must speak with Eclipse and Lunar," he said

finally. "This decision affects all three of us, and there are strategic considerations regarding Milano's interest in our presence."

Dani nodded, accepting his response without argument. "Okay. But promise me something?"

"What?"

"Don't leave without saying goodbye." Her voice remained steady, but Solar detected subtle changes in her energy pattern that suggested emotional vulnerability. "If you decide to go, I want to know. No disappearing acts."

"I will not depart without informing you," Solar promised, recognizing the importance of this commitment to her. "Regardless of the final decision, you deserve direct communication."

"Good." Dani leaned forward and pressed her lips to his, a brief contact that nevertheless sent energy spiraling through his system. "Now finish your coffee before it gets cold. Then we can figure out how to disguise a glowing alien long enough to get you back to your friends."

Solar complied, finding the cooling beverage less appealing but still functional as an energy source. He put his finger into it and caused the liquid to come to a rolling boil. Much better.

As he drank, he watched Dani move around the

apartment, gathering clothing and offering suggestions for concealing his true form.

Her adaptability impressed him. Most beings would react with fear or confusion to the revelation of alien life, yet Dani approached the situation with practical problem-solving and humor. It was a warrior's response, facing unexpected circumstances with calm assessment rather than emotional chaos.

"There's a hooded sweatshirt in my closet that should fit you," she called from the other room. "With sunglasses, we might be able to get you across town without causing a scene."

Solar set aside the empty mug and rose from the bed, his natural golden light now clearly visible beneath his skin. The complete failure of the skin-suit created tactical disadvantages, but he found himself unconcerned by the vulnerability. Here, with Dani, concealment seemed unnecessary.

A memory surfaced from his training. Adaptation to changing battlefield conditions was the mark of a superior warrior.

This situation was not a combat in the traditional sense, but it certainly required adaptation. Milano's hunters, Galaxy Brides' extraction timeline, and his own unexpected connection to an Earth female were all variables requiring strategic reassessment.

Dani returned with clothing, her expression determined. "These should work. The hoodie is extra large, and these sunglasses are the darkest I've got."

Solar accepted the offerings, examining them with curiosity. The garment was black with faded text across the front reading, *"Firewalker Festival 2019."* The material was soft but substantial enough to block some of his light emissions.

"This will restrict visibility," he observed, holding up the dark glasses.

"That's kind of the point," Dani replied with a smile. "Better for you to bump into things occasionally than for everyone to see you're literally glowing from within. Around here, you can get away with looking like you have body paint and tattoos as long as you limit the swirling beneath your skin, but your eyes will give you away. I swear they hold an entire universe inside of them. Human eyes could never do that."

Solar conceded the logic and began dressing in the Earth clothing. The loose-fitting garments were more comfortable than he expected, though still restrictive compared to the freedom of his natural state. Once fully clothed, with the hood pulled forward and the dark glasses in place, he turned to Dani for assessment.

Her expression was a mixture of amusement and approval. "Not bad. You look like a hungover rock star trying to avoid paparazzi."

"This is an effective disguise?" Solar asked skeptically.

"In Duskrock? Absolutely. Half the tourists here are trying to look mysterious and spiritual." She approached, adjusting the hood slightly. "Just keep your hands in your pockets and try not to set anything on fire."

"I maintain precise control of my thermal emissions," Solar informed her with dignity.

"Tell that to my curtains." Dani nodded toward the window, where the edge of one panel showed distinct scorch marks.

Solar had no memory of causing this damage, but given the intensity of their activities the previous night, some unintentional energy discharge was not implausible. "I will pay for replacements. They gave us Earth currency. I do not need it."

"Don't worry about it." Dani waved dismissively. "I'm considering it a souvenir. How many women can say their curtains were singed during alien sex?"

Her casual acceptance of such damage puzzled Solar. On Zorveya, resource efficiency was paramount, and any destruction, even accidental, required formal compensation. Yet another difference between their worlds.

"I should contact Eclipse immediately," Solar said, refocusing on tactical priorities. "Milano's interest creates danger for all three of us."

"Use my phone," Dani offered, retrieving the device from a table. "Does Eclipse have a cell number?"

"We were not provided with Earth communication technology," Solar admitted. "But the retreat where Rowan works should be able to connect us."

Dani nodded, quickly looking up the number and placing the call. After a brief conversation, she handed the phone to Solar.

"They're patching us through to the Desert Suite," she explained.

After several moments of silence, Eclipse's voice came through the device. "This is Eclipse."

"Solar," he identified himself. "We have a situation. Galaxy Brides has made contact. Milano Enterprises is tracking us."

There was a brief pause before Eclipse responded, his voice lowered. "We are aware. Rowan was approached by a Milano representative last night."

"They have accelerated the extraction timeline,"

Solar continued, summarizing Gary's communication. "Forty-eight hours at coordinates I will transmit separately. We must decide our response."

"Agreed. Return to the suite. Lunar must be informed as well." Eclipse's tone carried the familiar diplomatic caution Solar had come to expect. "This development changes our mission parameters significantly."

"I will arrive shortly," Solar confirmed before ending the call. He turned to Dani, who had been listening with obvious concern. "I must go to the retreat. Eclipse and I need to coordinate our response to this threat."

"I'm coming with you," Dani said immediately, already gathering her keys.

Solar considered objecting on tactical grounds, but quickly recognized the advantages of her assistance. She had local knowledge, transportation capabilities, and direct experience with his true form, which could prove valuable if his disguise failed.

"Your assistance would be appreciated," he acknowledged.

Dani smiled, clearly pleased by his acceptance. "Let me get dressed. We can stop for breakfast burritos on the way."

"Is food consumption a priority in this tactical

situation?" Solar asked, genuinely curious about her reasoning.

"Food is always a priority," Dani replied as she pulled on jeans and a t-shirt. "Especially when planning how to avoid shadowy government organizations hunting aliens. Plus, I'm starving after last night."

Solar could not argue with her logic. Energy replenishment was indeed a strategic necessity, particularly given the unknown demands they might face in the coming hours. And the memory of their night together created a warm surge in his energy field that momentarily brightened his golden glow beneath the concealing clothes.

7

Within minutes of leaving her home, they were in Dani's vehicle, moving through the streets of Duskrock toward the retreat. Solar kept his hood forward and his head down, minimizing exposure while maintaining awareness of their surroundings. His combat instincts remained active, scanning for potential threats or surveillance.

The small restaurant where Dani stopped was crowded, forcing Solar to maintain careful control of his energy emissions as they waited for their food at a small window. He noticed several humans watching him with curiosity as they passed the vehicle, though none approached.

"People are staring," he noted quietly to Dani.

"Because you look suspicious as hell," she replied

with a small smile. "But in Duskrock, that's practically normal. Nobody's calling the alien hunters yet."

He looked behind them and found a cowboy hat in the backseat. Taking it, he placed it on his head and pulled the brim down to shadow his face. People stopped staring as much. This disguise appeared to be functioning adequately, if not optimally.

Once they had acquired the food, which was wrapped in parcels containing egg, meat, and vegetable matter in a soft bread covering, they continued toward the retreat. Solar found the breakfast burrito surprisingly acceptable, converting the nutrients efficiently despite the unfamiliar composition.

As they drove, Dani glanced at him repeatedly, her expression growing increasingly thoughtful.

"So what are you going to do?" she finally asked. "About the extraction?"

Solar considered his response carefully. The tactical assessment was complex, with variables he had not anticipated when beginning this mission.

"I don't know," he admitted. "The logical course would be to follow extraction protocols and return to Zorveya. But..."

"But?" Dani prompted when he didn't continue.

"But my experience here has created unexpected

value propositions," Solar said, struggling to articulate concepts he had never needed to consider before. "Your energy signature, specifically, represents a resource unavailable on Zorveya."

Dani smiled slightly. "I think you just said I'm special."

"Your interpretation is accurate," Solar confirmed.

Her smile widened, but her eyes remained serious. "Special enough to stay for?"

The question crystallized the decision Solar had been processing since Gary's communication. Remaining on Earth meant abandoning his position in the Solarus Elite Guard, potentially cutting ties with his homeworld permanently. Yet returning to Zorveya meant leaving behind the unique connection he had formed with Dani, a connection that had already altered his understanding of energy exchange and interpersonal dynamics.

"I must consider all tactical variables," he said finally. "Including the danger Milano represents and the unknown intentions of the council that sent us here."

"That's not really an answer," Dani pointed out.

"No," Solar agreed. "It is not."

They arrived at the Duskrock Yoga and Spa

Meditation Center, pulling into a visitor space near the main building. Solar adjusted his disguise, ensuring maximum coverage before exiting the vehicle.

"Stay close," Dani advised. "Act like you belong here."

They moved through the entrance and toward the private areas, Dani confidently leading the way as if she had every right to be there. Solar maintained close proximity, his combat senses alert for any sign of threat or surveillance.

A human female approached them in the corridor, her expression curious. "Wait, stop! Can I help you?"

"We're heading to the Desert Suite," Dani replied smoothly. "Rowan's expecting us."

The female looked skeptical. "I'll need to check that. Visitors are supposed to sign in at reception."

Before Dani could respond, another female appeared from a side corridor. Solar recognized her as Stephanie, the loud one from their first day at the retreat.

"It's fine, Monica," Stephanie interjected. "They're with Rowan's private group. I just spoke to her. They're the VIPs in the Desert Suite."

Solar tensed, his hand instinctively moving

toward a weapon he wasn't carrying. Energy built, ready to surge if he needed to fight. Did this human know his designation?

Monica hesitated, then nodded. "Alright. But remember to use the sign-in system next time."

"Leave the VIPs alone, Monica. Celebrity stalking is how you get fired," Stephanie said. "Now, help me figure out where these aliens might be hiding."

"Not that again," Monica muttered. "I thought you said the aliens were the VIPs."

"Like Rowan would hang out with aliens," Stephenie laughed. "I like to tease her, but I can barely get her to leave the house on a weekend. She'd never do anything that exciting."

"Well, I think you're wasting your time," Monica quipped. "There is no such thing as aliens."

"Honey, I was there when they crash-landed. Got it all on video." Stephanie tapped her phone and held it up to Monica. "Did you see it yet? It's viral. Once I find them, I'm thinking book deal. Maybe a documentary series."

"Relax," Dani whispered.

Stephanie didn't realize he was an alien. He kept his head down as Dani pulled him with her.

Solar remained cautious. He needed it to stay

that way. That human's knowledge represented a potential security breach.

Dani led him through service corridors until they reached an exterior path that wound through gardens toward a separate structure built into the red rock. Solar maintained vigilance throughout the journey, aware that Milano could have operatives anywhere.

The Desert Suite was impressive by Earth standards, its design allowing it to blend with the natural landscape while providing strategic defensibility through limited access points.

After a moment, the door opened to reveal Eclipse, now wearing Earth clothing but with visible evidence of his true nature around his eyes and hands, where the twilight energy of his form leaked through.

"Eclipse," Solar acknowledged.

"Solar," he greeted with obvious relief. "Your disguise is effective."

"Yes. It is," Solar replied, moving past him into the suite. "I am a cowboy."

Rowan shared a look with Dani before turning to him. "I'm glad you're all right."

"We need to discuss Milano and the extraction timeline," Solar said, removing the concealing glasses now that they were in secure quarters. "Where is Lunar?"

"Unknown," Eclipse admitted. "He did not return last night."

"Hopefully still with Poppy," Rowan suggested. "I just texted her again to let her know Milano is at the retreat. I told them to be careful."

Solar frowned. Lunar's absence complicated tactical planning. "We must locate him immediately. Milano is actively tracking us, and Galaxy Brides has set extraction for forty-eight hours from now."

"They contacted you?" Rowan asked, her expression concerned.

"A Milano representative approached us at dinner last night," Eclipse said. "James Petersen. He mentioned unusual atmospheric disturbances and electromagnetic anomalies."

"They're using satellite technology and ground teams with specialized equipment," Solar added, relaying Gary's information.

"That tracks with what I uncovered before they shut down my investigation," Rowan nodded. "The Milano Foundation has been funding unusual research for years, supposedly for medical applications, but the security around their facilities was military-grade."

"So what's the plan?" Dani asked, looking between them. "Are you guys leaving?"

The question hung in the air, heavy with implications. She was not satisfied with the answers he'd given her. Then again, neither was he. Solar glanced at Eclipse, noting the subtle change in his energy pattern at the mention of departure.

"That decision has not been finalized," Eclipse said carefully. "We must discuss all options once Lunar is located."

"I can call Poppy," Dani offered, already pulling out her phone. "They're probably at her place. It's out near Boynton Canyon."

Rowan nodded. "Yeah, do that. I texted her, but maybe you'll have better luck."

As Dani made the call, Solar moved to the window, scanning the exterior for any sign of surveillance or unusual activity. The sunlight filtering through the glass energized his system, causing his golden light to brighten beneath the concealing clothing.

"Any sign of Galaxy Brides since their communication?" Eclipse asked quietly, joining him at the window.

"None," Solar confirmed. "Their sudden reappearance after abandoning us does not inspire confidence. As is the accelerated extraction timeline."

"My assessment as well," Eclipse agreed. "Their concern seems less for our welfare and more for avoiding complications with authorities."

"Or perhaps the council instructed them to retrieve us before we could form connections that might cause this mission to be deemed a success," Solar suggested. His gaze shifted briefly to Dani, who was engaged in conversation with Rowan across the room.

Eclipse followed his line of sight. "You have formed such a connection."

It wasn't a question, but Solar answered anyway. "Her energy signature creates resonance patterns unlike any I have encountered on Zorveya. The compatibility is significant."

"As is Rowan's with mine," Eclipse said. "I admit I did not think these developments were possible."

"Because the mission was never meant to succeed," Solar concluded, voicing the suspicion that had been growing since their arrival. "We were meant to be removed from Zorveya, not to prove coexistence is possible. They want this mission to fail."

"The evidence supports that hypothesis," Eclipse agreed solemnly. "What happened to your skin suit?"

"All but dissolved. Dani hid the remnants in her home."

Dani's voice interrupted their conversation. "Good news and bad news. I reached Poppy, and Lunar is with her. That's the good news."

"And the bad?" Rowan asked.

"They spotted men in black SUVs near her place this morning. Professional types with equipment. They're hiding out in some cave system Poppy knows."

Solar and Eclipse exchanged glances, the tactical implications immediately clear to both.

"Milano has begun active pursuit," Solar stated.

"Poppy says she can bring Lunar here tonight after dark," Dani continued. "But they're staying put until then. Something about him being more mobile at night?"

"His shadow-walking abilities are enhanced in darkness," Eclipse explained. "A wise precaution."

"So what do we do until then?" Dani asked, the practical question cutting through the tension.

Solar considered their options. "We prepare defenses, gather intelligence on Milano's activities, and develop contingency plans for multiple scenarios."

"I can help with the intelligence part," Rowan offered. "I still have contacts who might know what Milano is up to locally."

Solar nodded. These Earth females were proving to be valuable allies, adapting quickly to the situation despite its unprecedented nature.

"We should also prepare for the possibility that Galaxy Brides' extraction may be compromised," he added. "If Milano has tracking capability for alien technology, they may detect any attempt to remove us from Earth."

"So we're talking about a potential showdown," Dani summarized. "Aliens versus shadowy government contractors."

"A scenario I had hoped to avoid," Eclipse admitted. "Our mission was supposed to be peaceful cultural exchange."

"Sometimes peace isn't an option," Solar replied, the warrior in him recognizing the approaching conflict. "Sometimes you must fight to protect what matters."

His gaze met Dani's, and in that moment, Solar knew his decision was already made, regardless of tactical assessments or mission parameters. He had found something on Earth worth protecting, worth fighting for. If Milano or Galaxy Brides threatened that connection, they would discover firsthand why the warriors of the Solarus Elite Guard were feared across multiple star systems.

The sun continued its arc across the Earth sky, its light strengthening Solar's resolve along with his energy reserves. Whatever came next, he would face it with the full radiance of his true nature, no longer constrained by diplomatic caution or concealing membranes.

Let them come. Solar was ready.

8

Dani had survived plenty of bad situations in her life—foster homes with locks on the refrigerators, sleeping in bus terminals when she ran out of money, and that one boyfriend who thought "fire dancer" meant "girl who likes getting burned." But being hunted by a shady corporation with alien-tracking technology? This was a new one.

"Act normal," Rowan murmured as they stepped out of the Desert Suite into the blinding Arizona sun.

Dani forced a laugh like Rowan had said something hilarious, nodding at a group of tourists snapping photos by the meditation garden. "What exactly is normal when you're hiding glowing alien boyfriends from men in black?"

"Just look like you belong," Rowan replied

through her perfect customer service smile. Her eyes suddenly fixed on something across the courtyard. "Don't look now, but security guy at two o'clock. Earpiece, tactical stance, trying too hard to blend in."

Rowan was beginning to sound like the aliens. This wasn't some military role-playing game. It was real life, and she was terrified. Dani resisted the urge to spin around. Instead, she pretended to be fascinated by a nearby cactus while stealing a glance in her peripheral vision. The man stood, his gaze moving methodically over the grounds. "Got it."

Her pulse quickened. This wasn't some rent-a-cop resort security. This was professional.

"So what's our actual plan here?" Dani asked, keeping her voice light. "Just stroll around and hope they don't grab us?"

"Basically," Rowan admitted. "But we need to—"

A high-pitched electronic whine cut through the air. Dani looked up instinctively, and her stomach dropped. A sleek black drone hovered overhead, its camera lens adjusting as it focused directly on them.

"Shit," she whispered. "I think our cover's blown. That didn't take long."

"Keep walking," Rowan urged. "If they wanted to grab us, they would have already."

Easy for her to say. Dani had left Solar back in

that suite, vulnerable and exposed. Her hand twitched, fingers curling as if she could somehow reach through space and pull him to safety. She'd only known him for days, but the thought of Milano getting their hands on him made her physically sick.

The drone followed their movement like a patient predator, maintaining a consistent distance as they continued toward the pool area. Guests lounged in the morning sun, oblivious to the fact that they were sharing space with actual aliens and the people hunting them.

"They're herding us," Rowan said, her voice tense.

"What?"

"They're channeling us away from the Desert Suite." Rowan's eyes darted around, taking in the positions of men who suddenly looked less like maintenance workers and more like operatives. "They want to separate us from Solar and Eclipse."

How could Rowan possibly know that? She was in retreat management. Wasn't she? Suddenly, the woman was acting like some kind of trained spy.

Rowan's phone buzzed. She glanced at the screen and showed Dani a text from an unknown number, *"Ms. Clark. Please proceed to the front entrance. Mr. Petersen would like a word."*

"They're tracking your phone," Dani said, feeling a rush of adrenaline. "We need to ditch it."

"No," Rowan replied, her fingers already typing a response. "We need to use it."

Dani watched as Rowan bought them time with a bogus reply. She'd underestimated this woman. Beneath the yoga retreat coordinator's exterior was someone who clearly knew how to handle pressure.

"Now we need to move. Fast," Rowan said, steering them toward a small garden shed.

Once inside the cramped, chlorine-scented space, Dani's mind raced. "Okay, so we've established that Milano has the place surrounded. Can we go back now?"

Every second away from Solar felt like torture.

"Not yet." Rowan peered through the small window and seemed to be counting Milano operatives. "We need to figure out how many they have and what kind of equipment they're using. If we go straight back, they'll just follow us to Eclipse and Solar."

A metallic clank sounded on the roof. Both women froze.

"I think they're scanning for us," Rowan whispered. "If they've developed technology to track the aliens..."

The drone emitted a sharp electronic beep, and Dani's blood ran cold. They'd been found.

"We need to move. Now." Rowan grabbed a pool skimmer from the wall and shoved the door open, swinging the pole upward in one fluid motion.

The drone sputtered as its propellers caught in the net, careening sideways and crashing into a cactus.

"Run!" Rowan shouted.

Dani's body reacted before her mind could process, legs pumping as she sprinted after Rowan across the pool deck. Her years of martial arts training kicked in, her breathing controlled despite the surge of panic. Behind them, men shouted, abandoning all pretense of covert operations.

Dani glanced back, and her heart jumped. Three men were gaining on them, reaching inside their jackets for what looked suspiciously like weapons. She veered sharply left, spotting the open-air yoga pavilion.

"This way!"

Twenty peaceful yogis stretched in warrior pose as Dani and Rowan power-walked through their midst.

"Sorry, maintenance emergency," Rowan called to the bewildered instructor.

The Milano men halted at the edge, as if unwilling to cause a scene with so many witnesses. Thank goodness for small victories.

As soon as they cleared the pavilion, they broke into a run again. The muscles in Dani's legs burned, but fear drove her forward. She'd spent her life running—*from foster homes, from relationships, from commitment*—but this was the first time she'd run toward something worth fighting for.

"We can't lead them back to the suite," she managed through heavy breaths, thinking of Solar.

"I know," Rowan panted. "We need to split up."

They reached a junction in the path. Ahead lay the main building with a narrow trail that wound toward the red rocks at the property's edge.

"Take the trail," Rowan instructed. "Circle around the canyon side. I'll create a diversion."

"What? No!" Dani protested, grabbing Rowan's arm. "They're after you specifically."

"Exactly." Rowan pulled away, already backing toward the main building. "I'll be fine. Get to Eclipse and Solar. Tell them Milano is actively hunting us, not just watching. Don't contact my phone. Don't come after me."

Before Dani could argue further, Rowan turned and sprinted toward the retreat's central building.

Something about her confidence made Dani think this wasn't her first time evading pursuit.

Dani hesitated for one precious second before darting down the narrow trail. The red rock path rose steadily, snaking around natural formations and offering sparse vegetation for cover. Her lungs burned with the exertion, but she pushed on, scanning constantly for signs of pursuit.

She'd made it halfway up the trail when movement below caught her eye. Three Milano operatives were spreading out at the trail's base, speaking into their comms. They hadn't spotted her yet, but it was only a matter of time.

Dani dropped to a crouch behind a twisted juniper, her heart hammering against her ribs. She needed to circle back to the suite, but these guys were blocking the obvious route. She'd have to go higher, find another way around.

The path steepened as she climbed, loose rocks skittering beneath her feet. A misstep sent a cascade of pebbles down the slope. She froze, pressing herself against the cliff face as one of the men below looked up, scanning the trail.

For an excruciating moment, Dani didn't breathe. The operative stared directly at her position, then, seemingly satisfied, returned to his surveillance. She exhaled slowly, her hands trembling slightly.

Keep moving. Keep moving. Keep moving.

The mantra repeated in her head as she picked her way higher. From this elevation, she could see more of the retreat's layout. The main building swarmed with activity. Rowan's diversion was working. But to her horror, she spotted black SUVs pulling up to the Desert Suite. Men in tactical gear poured out, surrounding the building.

Solar.

They'd found him.

Her entire body trembled in fear. The thought of him captured, experimented on, and dissected. It sent a wave of nausea through her. She needed to warn him, somehow.

A distant commotion drew her attention to the main entrance. A colorful parade of... What the hell? People in alien costumes? A man with a bullhorn led the group, his silver jumpsuit catching the sun as he gestured dramatically. Behind him, at least thirty people in various extraterrestrial getups waved signs and shouted slogans.

"The truth is here!" boomed across the retreat grounds.

Dani recognized Pete from the crystal shop, his

wispy gray hair flying as he directed his flash mob of alien enthusiasts straight toward the Milano operatives. Several confused tourists joined the parade, thinking it was part of the retreat's entertainment.

Rowan must have called in reinforcements. Clever girl.

The distraction gave Dani her opening. As Milano personnel moved to contain the unexpected Earth-alien invasion, she darted across an exposed section of trail to a service path that wound behind the guest cottages. From there, she could approach the Desert Suite from the rear.

She was halfway there when a deafening crash echoed across the grounds. Dani whipped around to see the front door of the Desert Suite flying off its hinges. Smoke billowed out, followed by a flash of golden light so bright it left spots in her vision.

No!

Solar.

A surge of something—*electricity?*—arced from inside the suite, followed by screams. Two Milano operatives stumbled out, their tactical gear smoking. One collapsed to his knees, the other dragged him away from the door.

More operatives rushed forward, carrying strange weapons that bore no resemblance to conventional firearms. Dani's heart lodged in her throat. Whatever they were planning, she couldn't let them hurt Solar.

She sprinted toward the suite, abandoning stealth for speed. Twenty yards out, she spotted movement on the ridge above. Three figures were climbing rapidly away from the suite. Even from this distance, she recognized Solar's golden glow and Eclipse's twilight shimmer. Rowan was with them, leading them up a narrow trail.

They'd escaped. Relief flooded through her, immediately followed by dread. Where did that leave her?

More Milano personnel poured out of the suite, pointing up at the escaping trio. Several raised weapons. Dani changed direction, ducking behind landscaping to avoid detection. If she followed Solar's group now, she'd only lead Milano straight to them.

A hand clamped over her mouth from behind.

Dani reacted instantly, driving her elbow back hard. There was a satisfying grunt of pain as her attacker loosened their grip. She spun, dropping into a fighting stance.

A man in a silver alien costume held up his hands, wincing. "Jesus, lady. Pete sent me!"

Dani stared at him, recognition dawning. "Tommy? From the fire safety demos?"

"Yeah." He rubbed his ribs where she'd struck him. "Pete sent me to find you. Said you might need extraction."

Dani glanced back at the chaos surrounding the Desert Suite. Milano operatives were organizing into search teams, some heading toward the trail Solar and the others had taken.

"I need to follow them," she said, pointing to the ridge.

Tommy shook his head. "Bad idea. Those guys have the trail covered. Pete says to come with us. We've got a plan."

"What kind of plan?"

Tommy grinned and pulled something from his backpack He held up an alien costume complete with a large-headed mask. "Hiding in plain sight."

Five minutes later, Dani danced along with Pete's alien flash mob, her face concealed behind a rubber mask, her body draped in a silver jumpsuit. The costume was hot and smelled like someone else's sweat, but it worked. Milano operatives glared at them but were too busy organizing their pursuit to detain random cosplayers.

Pete sidled up next to her, his alien mask pushed up to reveal his bearded face. "Rowan called in the cavalry," he explained proudly. "Code Green. Been waiting years for this moment."

"Have you seen them?" Dani asked urgently.

"I got reports they went into the caves," Pete replied. "Smart move. Those tunnels branch for miles. Milano's guys will be lost for days without local guides."

A thunderous boom echoed from the direction of the ridge, and everyone turned to look. A plume of dust rose from an opening in the rock face.

"What the hell was that?" Dani gasped.

"Nothing good," Pete replied grimly. "Those caves are unstable if you don't know what you're doing."

Dani's stomach twisted. Solar was powerful, but she doubted that cave-ins discriminated between humans and aliens. "I need to get up there."

"No can do, little missy," Pete said, gripping her arm firmly. "Milano's got the trails locked down tight. But I have a better idea. Come on."

He led her through the crowd toward the retreat's parking lot, where his ancient VW van waited, painted with cosmic scenes and crystal formations. The side panel bore the logo of Pete's Crystal Emporium in psychedelic lettering.

"Pete, I got it!" A man painted green from head to toe and wearing a pink tutu rushed forward carrying a knapsack. "I grabbed everything I could find."

"Good work, Marvin!" Pete praised, opening the side door of his van.

Dani hesitated.

"Get in," Pete instructed. "We're going around to the other side of the canyon. There's another cave entrance there. If your friends know what they're doing, that's where they'll come out."

Dani climbed in. She had no choice but to trust them, which was not exactly her strong suit.

The interior smelled of incense and marijuana. Crystals dangled from the rearview mirror. A few of Pete's fellow enthusiasts piled in behind her, still in their alien costumes. Others remained outside, their flash mob having turned into an impromptu party. They were joined by several retreat guests still wearing their yoga gear.

"Full disclosure," Pete said as he started the engine. "I've been waiting my whole life to help real aliens escape government persecution. This is basically my Super Bowl."

Under different circumstances, Dani might have laughed. Instead, she stared out the window as the van pulled away, watching Milano reinforcements arrive at the retreat. Solar was out there somewhere, possibly injured, definitely hunted.

"Faster," she urged Pete. "Please."

The van rumbled along the main road before turning onto a dirt track that wound around the canyon's perimeter.

"Marv, what'd you get?" Pete asked.

Marvin began pulling items from his bag and piling them next to Pete on the center console. Tiny liquor bottles clanked.

"Oo, refreshments!" one of the guys in the back seat reached over and grabbed a couple of bottles.

Next came packages of cookies.

"Dammit, Marv, this is serious! Did you go to the right room?" Pete yelled, even though his voice carried easily over the van's interior.

Marvin reached to pull the cookies back. Pete quickly snatched them and put them on his lap. "I'll take those."

"I got the good stuff," Marvin insisted. He pulled out a small device that looked to be alien tech.

Dani snatched it from him. "What are you doing with that? That's not yours."

"Keeping it out of the wrong hands," Marvin said defensively.

"Give her the goods," Pete ordered.

"That's what I was trying to do before you started yelling at me," Marvin defended. "I got in there before those super soldiers had a chance to get back. But I also couldn't let all those little bottles go to waste. We can sell them online. Booty straight from the aliens' room! I had to get the extra supplies out—"

"Let me see." Dani snatched the bag from him and looked inside. More tech devices were there, along with a black stone. "Good job, Marvin. This is great work. Very helpful."

Marvin grinned. "Did you hear that? I did great work. Saved the day, I did! Make sure you spell my name right for the record, Pete."

Dani wasn't sure she believed in crystal energy, but right now, she'd take any help she could get. A week ago, she didn't believe she'd ever meet an alien. Her hand closed around what she thought was a black stone. She felt a soft vibration, and it was pliable against her palm. This wasn't a normal rock.

"Almost there," Pete announced as the van bounced over ruts in the trail.

Another distant boom shook the ground, stronger than the first. Dani's knuckles whitened as she gripped the dashboard. "What's happening in there?"

"Either Milano brought explosives," Pete replied

grimly, "or your alien friends are putting up one hell of a fight."

The van lurched to a stop at a small clearing surrounded by twisted junipers. A narrow path led toward the red rock face, where a dark opening was barely visible behind scrub brush.

"Cavern's back there," Pete said. "Connects to the main system. If they're following the water channels, they'll come out here or at Twisted Point about half a mile north."

Dani was out of the van before he finished speaking, pulling off the cumbersome alien costume. "I need to go in."

"Whoa, bad idea," Pete warned. "Those caves are a maze unless you know them. And after those explosions, there could be collapse points."

"I don't care," Dani said, her voice steady despite the fear churning inside her. "Solar's in there." She met Pete's eyes with a determination that brooked no argument. "I'm going in."

Pete studied her for a moment, then sighed. "You're either the bravest or craziest person I've met. And I run an alien conspiracy shop in Duskrock."

He reached into the van and pulled out a backpack.

"Take this. Flashlight, water, basic first aid. And

this." He handed her a weathered paper map. "It's an old survey of the cave system. Not complete, but better than nothing."

Dani took the supplies with a grateful nod. She shoved Marvin's knapsack into the bag. "Thank you. For everything."

"Just bring them back safe," Pete replied. "I've got questions about the cosmos that need answering."

Dani approached the cave entrance, flashlight in hand. The darkness yawned before her, cool air wafting from its depths. She'd never been afraid of the dark, but this wasn't just darkness. It was unknown territory where the man she was falling for might be fighting for his life.

She took a deep breath and stepped inside. The temperature dropped immediately, the smell of earth and minerals filling her nostrils. Her flashlight beam cut through the gloom, revealing a passage that sloped downward. Water dripped somewhere in the distance.

"Solar!" she called out, hoping she didn't draw the wrong attention. The only response was her voice echoing back at her from within the cave.

9

What the hell was she doing?

This was the very definition of stupid.

There had to be, what? Miles of cave systems? Did she really think she could feel her way to Solar's energy?

Something inside her told her she had to try. She'd never forgive herself if she didn't.

The deeper Dani ventured into the cave, the colder it became. Her flashlight beam bounced eerily off the damp walls, revealing strange formations that cast distorted shadows. Water dripped somewhere in the distance, a steady metronome counting down seconds she didn't have to waste.

"Solar!" she called again softly, her voice met by

the darkness. She willed his glow to show her the way to him.

No reply. Just her own echo, mocking her.

She told herself she could turn around and make her way back to the entrance at any time. That was before the cave veered in two different directions and then two more.

Dani pulled Pete's map from her backpack, shining the light on the weathered paper. Faded lines and cryptic markings offered little guidance to someone who'd never been caving before. According to Pete, if Solar and the others were following water channels, they'd emerge either here or half a mile north. But the map showed a maze of interconnected tunnels between her current position and either exit.

"Okay, think," she muttered to herself. "What would Solar do? Where would I go if I were an alien in need of sunlight to fuel myself?"

He'd follow the most direct route, she decided. Like him, light traveled in straight lines when possible. She traced a path on the map with her finger, finding what looked like a main passage that led deeper into the system before branching toward both potential exits. It wasn't much, but it was a plan.

And that was if Solar was guiding the others. She had no clue what Eclipse or Rowan would do. Or where they'd go. And then there was Milano. Who knew which direction they would chase them?

Shit. Shit. Shit.

What should she do?

Dani moved forward, careful of her footing on the slick cave floor. She hated the cold darkness. The passage narrowed, forcing her to turn sideways at points. The rough rock scraped against her back, leaving her shirt damp from the moisture seeping through the stone.

A distant boom shook the cave, stronger than the ones she'd heard outside. Dust and small rocks rained down, forcing her to cover her head.

"Solar," she quietly pleaded, genuine fear creeping into her voice. She wanted to yell but what if he wasn't the one to answer?

The tunnel widened into a chamber where several passages branched off in different directions. Dani consulted the map again, but in the dim light, the faded lines blurred together. She was running on instinct now.

Too bad her instincts knew very little about caves.

Something caught her attention. She saw a faint scorch mark on the wall of one passage, as if something very hot had brushed against it. Solar?

It was the best clue she had.

Dani hurried down that tunnel, hope pushing her forward. The passage sloped downward, the air growing damper. The sound of running water grew louder until she emerged into a larger chamber where a stream cut across her path.

She played her flashlight across the water. According to Pete's map, following this stream would eventually lead to one of the exits. However, there was no indication of which direction to take. Upstream or down?

A soft glow emanating from upstream caught her eye. Too steady to be a flashlight, too golden to be anything but...

"Solar," she breathed, breaking into a jog along the streambank.

The glow disappeared around a bend. Dani quickened her pace, splashing through shallow parts of the stream where the path narrowed. She rounded the corner and stopped short.

The chamber ahead was empty. The golden light was gone.

"I saw you," she called, frustration edging her voice. "Solar, if that's you, please."

Nothing. She must have imagined it.

Tears filled her eyes. Dani consulted the map

again and looked around. She thought about turning back.

This stream should lead toward the northern exit, if she was reading it correctly. She decided to continue upstream.

The path grew treacherous, forcing her to wade through knee-deep water at points. The cold seeped through her jeans, numbing her legs. Her teeth chattered, but she pushed on.

Another boom echoed through the cave, closer this time. The ground shook violently, throwing Dani off balance. She stumbled, her foot slipping on wet stone. Her ankle twisted painfully as she fell sideways into the stream.

Icy water engulfed her, shocking the breath from her lungs. The current, stronger than it appeared, began dragging her downstream. Her waterlogged backpack pulled her down. The flashlight slipped from her grasp, its beam dancing wildly across the cave ceiling before disappearing.

Darkness swallowed her as the current accelerated. Dani fought against panic, forcing herself to think clearly. She managed to get her feet under her, pushing off the rocky bottom to break the surface. She gasped for air, choking on water that splashed into her mouth.

"Help!" she cried, knowing it was futile. No one could hear her.

The stream curved sharply, sending her crashing into a rock wall. Pain exploded in her shoulder, but adrenaline kept her moving. She grabbed at passing rocks, her fingers scraping against the rough surface until she finally caught hold of a jutting stone.

Clinging to the rock, Dani pulled herself toward the bank, fighting the current. Her muscles screamed with effort as she dragged herself onto a narrow ledge.

She lay there gasping, soaked and shivering in the pitch darkness. The map was gone, along with the flashlight. The soaked backpack pulled heavily against her shoulders.

"Stupid," she berated herself. "So stupid."

Years of martial arts training had taught Dani to respect each opponent, to never underestimate a challenge. She'd disrespected the cave, charged in without proper equipment or knowledge, and now she was paying for it.

Without light, ruined supplies, and no map, she was as good as dead. Every instinct screamed at her to turn back, to try to find her way to the entrance before hypothermia set in. It was the logical choice. The only choice, really.

Only, which way was back? The cave was dark, and the water had tossed her around.

This was how she was going to die.

Here. Alone. Terrified.

"What the fuck am I doing?" Dani pushed herself to a sitting position, wincing at the pain in her ankle and shoulder. "You're not dying in a cave today," she told herself firmly. "And you're not leaving without Solar."

Her eyes gradually adjusted to the darkness, revealing that it wasn't quite absolute. A faint ambient glow filtered through the cave system, perhaps from cracks in the ceiling or bioluminescent organisms. It wasn't much, but it was enough to make out basic shapes and avoid walking into walls.

She struggled to her feet, testing her injured ankle. It hurt like hell, but it supported her weight. Not broken, then. Just badly sprained.

Dani fumbled in her pocket, finding that her small lighter had survived the dunking. It wouldn't provide much light, but it was better than nothing.

Flicking the lighter, she created a small island of light. The flame revealed she was in a side chamber off the main stream passage. There was no way to tell which direction led out or deeper in.

A sound echoed faintly through the cave. Human voices.

Milano? She couldn't tell.

Dani extinguished the lighter immediately, pressing herself against the wall. The voices grew louder. There were at least two men, maybe three, their words indistinct but their tone clipped and punctuated by the static pops of walkie-talkies.

A beam of light swept across the chamber entrance. Dani held her breath, willing herself to become one with the shadows. The light paused, then continued on. The voices faded as the men moved away, following the stream.

She exhaled slowly. They were heading the same direction she had been, upstream toward where she thought she'd seen Solar's glow. If Milano was tracking in that direction, it suggested she might have been right about Solar's location.

Dani waited until she was certain they were gone before limping toward the chamber exit. She'd follow them at a distance, using their lights to guide her while staying out of sight.

Moving as quietly as her injured ankle allowed, Dani crept along the passage, keeping the distant flashlight beams in view. The Milano agents moved with purpose, as if following some kind of tracker.

The tunnel widened into another chamber with multiple exits. The men paused, consulting a device that emitted a soft blue glow. One of them pointed toward a passage on the far side, and they moved in that direction.

Dani waited until they disappeared before entering the chamber. Without their lights, the darkness closed in again. She flicked her lighter, revealing petroglyphs of spirals, stars, and humanoid figures with elongated heads on the walls.

A sudden overwhelming sense of being watched froze her in place. The flame wavered in her trembling hand as she slowly turned in a circle, searching the shadows.

"Who's there?" she whispered.

The darkness seemed to shift, coalescing into a deeper patch of black in one corner. A cold sensation prickled along Dani's spine.

"Lunar?" she hoped, her voice barely audible.

The darkness moved, flowing like liquid night until it formed a vaguely humanoid shape. "You should not be here," came a voice that seemed to emanate from the shadows themselves.

Relief flooded through Dani. She'd hug him if she could find his corporeal form. "Neither should you, but here we are." She gave a nervous laugh. "Where's Solar? Is he with you?"

"Not here," Lunar replied. "He and Eclipse were separated during Milano's attack. I tracked them through the cave system but lost their energy signatures near an underground stream. Then I felt the energy stone."

"The what?"

He came closer and touched her wet backpack. "What is this?"

"I fell into that stream," Dani admitted, thinking he meant the fact that she was wet. "The current carried me."

The shadow form shifted closer. "No, I feel the stone."

"Oh, yeah, we managed to salvage some of your alien stuff from the suite. I brought it." She started to take off the backpack, but winced as the weight adjusted on her shoulder.

"You are injured," Lunar stated.

"I'll live," she said dismissively. "You need to find Solar before they do. Get him to safety."

"Agreed," Lunar said. "But first, you require assistance. Poppy is securing an exit point. I will take you to her."

"Not without Solar," Dani insisted.

"You misunderstand." A note of impatience entered Lunar's cold voice. "I will continue tracking Solar and Eclipse after ensuring your safety. Your injured state makes you a liability in this environment, and your human movements slow me down."

Dani bristled at being called a liability, but couldn't deny the logic. Her ankle throbbed, her clothes were soaked, and she'd lost her flashlight and map. She was in no condition to continue searching.

"Fine," she conceded reluctantly. "But once I'm with Poppy, you find Solar and bring him back. Promise me."

The shadow form seemed to consider this. "I will locate him if possible."

It wasn't quite a promise, but it was the best she was going to get from him.

"We must move quickly. The Milano agents may double back at any moment," Lunar said. "We will shadow-walk."

"What—?"

Without warning, Lunar's shadow form enveloped Dani. The sensation was unlike anything she'd experienced. It felt like being wrapped in cold silk that somehow supported her weight. Her feet left the ground as Lunar carried her effortlessly through the darkness.

The shadow-walking was disorienting. Dani couldn't tell if they were moving through solid rock or following passages. There was no sense of direction, only of swift, silent movement through absolute darkness.

Then suddenly, natural daylight appeared ahead, filtering through a narrow opening. Lunar set her down gently as his form contracted back into a more humanoid shape.

"Wait here," he instructed. "Poppy is nearby."

Before Dani could respond, Lunar melted back into the shadows and disappeared.

She leaned against the cave wall, taking weight off her injured ankle. The opening was too small for her to exit without crawling, but fresh air flowed in, clearing the damp cave smell from her lungs.

Minutes later, a familiar face appeared at the opening.

"Dani," Poppy exclaimed, relief evident in her voice. "Thank goodness. Lunar said you need a doctor?"

"No. I just twisted my ankle," Dani downplayed, though she winced as she shifted her weight. "I'm more worried about Solar. Have you seen him?"

Poppy shook her head. "Not since the retreat.

Lunar's been tracking energy signatures through the caves, but Milano's equipment is interfering."

She helped Dani squeeze through the narrow opening, supporting her as they emerged onto a sun-baked ledge high on the canyon wall.

"Here, give me that," Poppy reached for the backpack.

"That's their tech," Dani said.

"What tech?" Poppy asked, steadying Dani as she stumbled.

"Rowan called Pete from the crystal shop to cause a distraction. Marvin, one of his alien enthusiast friends, managed to grab some items from the suite before Milano took over. Devices, something Lunar called an energy stone... I don't know what they do, but I figured they shouldn't fall into Milano's hands."

"Good thinking. Even seemingly innocuous alien tech could be dangerous if reverse-engineered," Poppy said, carrying the bag. "There's a jeep hidden about a quarter mile from here. We need to get moving. Milano's got helicopters searching the area."

As if on cue, the distant thump of rotors echoed across the canyon.

Poppy helped her along a narrow path that hugged the cliff face. They reached a point where the path widened, allowing them to move more quickly despite Dani's injury. In the distance, a black helicopter swept low over the canyon rim.

"Down," Poppy hissed, pulling Dani behind a large boulder.

They pressed themselves against the warm stone as the helicopter passed overhead, its shadow sliding across the ground. She bit her lip, trying not to cry out at the pain the sudden jarring motion caused. After the helicopter moved on, Poppy led them through a maze of rock formations until they reached a dry wash where an old jeep was hidden under a natural overhang.

"Nice ride," Dani commented.

"It knows these canyons better than any Milano SUV," Poppy replied with a hint of pride. She helped Dani into the passenger seat, then checked her ankle. "This needs ice."

She pulled a first aid kit from under the seat and found it empty. "Dammit. I forgot to restock."

"It'll be okay," Dani said, rubbing her calf as if to soothe the pain in her ankle. "What's the plan?"

"I know a place about twenty miles into the backcountry. Off-grid cabin, no electricity, no cell service. Milano won't find us there." Poppy glanced toward the cave entrance they'd emerged from. "I told Lunar we'd go there once he finds the others."

"If he finds them," Dani said quietly, voicing the fear that had been growing since she'd lost sight of that golden glow in the cave.

Poppy gave her shoulder a gentle squeeze. "He'll find them. Lunar may seem cold, but he's incredibly determined. And Solar strikes me as the type who'd burn through a mountain to get back to someone he cares about."

The sentiment brought a lump to Dani's throat. She'd only known Solar for a short while, but the thought of losing him felt like having her heart torn out. It wasn't just the amazing alien sex or the novelty of dating someone from another planet. There was something about his directness, his intensity, the way he saw her fire manipulation as art rather than entertainment.

"I need to go back in," Dani decided. "I can't just leave him in there. I have to do something."

"You can barely walk," Poppy pointed out. "And Milano's combing every inch of these canyons. The best thing we can do is secure a safe location for when they get out."

Logic warred with emotion as Dani stared back at the cave entrance. Poppy was right, damn her. Going back in with a busted ankle would only endanger herself and potentially Solar if he had to rescue her.

"Fine," she relented. "But we need supplies. Food, water, first aid. If they're injured when they get out..."

"Can you ride?" Poppy asked.

"Ride?" Dani raised an eyebrow.

"Crotch-rocket."

"Yeah, but..." She glanced around.

"Good. I'm taking you to the animal clinic. I'll drop you off and come back here to get the others. You wrap that ankle, stock up on first aid and supplies, then meet back up with us. The staff motorcycle is around the back of the building. Take it."

The helicopter returned, forcing them to duck down in the jeep until it passed. Once it was clear, Poppy started the engine.

"Hold tight," she warned. "This isn't going to be a smooth ride."

She wasn't kidding. The jeep bounced over the rugged terrain, each jolt sending spikes of pain through Dani's injured ankle. But Poppy drove with impressive skill, navigating between rock formations and along barely visible trails that seemed to disappear and reappear at random.

As they drove, Dani kept looking back toward the caves, searching for any sign of Solar's golden glow or

Eclipse's twilight shimmer against the red rocks. There was only the harsh sunlight and increasing distance.

"We'll find them," Poppy said, correctly interpreting Dani's backward glances.

Dani nodded, not trusting herself to speak. She turned her attention to the path ahead, watching as Poppy navigated the jeep down a nearly invisible track that wound deeper into the wilderness.

The sun was beginning its descent toward the horizon, painting the red rocks in deeper shades of crimson. Shadows lengthened across the landscape. This was Lunar's time.

"If anyone could find Solar and Eclipse in the darkness of those caves, it would be Lunar," Poppy assured her.

They drove in silence for ten minutes before coming up behind the animal clinic. As she slowed the vehicle, Poppy gave Dani directions on where to meet them.

Dani barely had time to get out before Poppy was speeding away. The jeep's dust cloud hung in the air long after the vehicle disappeared. Clutching the backpack of alien tech to her chest, Dani hobbled toward the back door of the clinic. Her ankle throbbed with every step, and her clothes were still damp from the cave stream. Behind the building, she spotted the motorcycle Poppy had mentioned. The battered but serviceable motorcycle had a half-tank of gas.

As she turned the key in the clinic's back door, she heard the distant thump of helicopter rotors. Milano was still hunting. Somewhere in those caves, Solar was fighting to survive. Dani took a deep breath and pushed inside. She'd patch herself up, gather supplies, and be ready when they found him.

Because they would find him. They had to.

10

Darkness.

Solar despised darkness. It was antithetical to his very existence.

Yet here he was, his natural radiance dimmed to conserve energy and hide his presence, huddled beside a human female in the oppressive gloom of an Earth cave. The irony was not lost on him. A warrior of the Solarus Elite Guard, a being of pure light and heat, reduced to hiding like a shadow-dweller.

"You're glowing again," Rowan whispered, her voice tight with strain.

Solar forced his energy to contract, pulling the golden light deeper beneath his skin. The effort was painful, like trying to fold a star into a matchbox. "Did you hear Milano's scanners?"

"I don't know," Rowan admitted. "But we can't risk it."

They had been moving through the cave system for what felt like hours, though Solar's internal chronometer suggested it had been less than ten Earth minutes since they'd become separated from Eclipse. The memory of that moment sent a surge of anger through his system, causing his skin to brighten involuntarily.

Eclipse had created a diversion, expanding his twilight energy to cover their escape while Milano's forces closed in. It was tactically sound but relied on the assumption that Eclipse could protect himself. Solar had his doubts. Those weapons had been specifically designed to counter their energy signatures.

But his most pressing concern was Dani's whereabouts. When Milano attacked the Desert Suite, she had been out with Rowan. Logic suggested she was safe, but logic provided little comfort against the visceral fear that had taken root in his system.

A distant rumble shook the cave, sending a shower of dust and small rocks pattering down around them. Solar instinctively brightened, creating a protective dome of energy over Rowan.

"Was that an explosion?" she gasped.

"Eclipse," Solar said grimly. "He must be using his twilight energy to distract them from our position."

The thought of what might be happening to Eclipse sent a fresh wave of anger through Solar's system. Despite their differences, Eclipse was a fellow Zorveyan. More than that, he was... Solar searched for the appropriate Earth term. A comrade. Perhaps even a friend, though Solar had little experience with such relationships outside of the guard.

"He's buying us time," Solar stated. "We need to make it count."

They pressed on, the cave system growing increasingly complex. Multiple passages branched off in different directions, some too narrow for comfortable passage, others sloping dangerously downward.

"Do you know where we're going?" Solar asked, noting Rowan's hesitation at each junction.

"Not exactly," she admitted. "I've hiked these canyons, but I've never gone deep into the cave system. I'm following the water and hoping it leads out."

Hope. Not the most strategic approach, but their options were limited. Solar expanded his senses, searching for any energy signature that might indicate an exit. Sunlight, fresh air currents, even the subtle electromagnetic fields of the outside world, anything to guide them.

"This way," he indicated a passage where a faint breeze could be detected. "Air flow suggests an opening."

They followed the new path, which gradually began to slope upward. Solar's energy reserves were depleting without direct solar radiation to replenish them. The constant suppression of his natural emissions taxed him further. Soon, he would be forced to either release his energy, potentially alerting Milano to their location, or risk losing his physical cohesion entirely.

Another explosion shook the cave, this one closer and more violent. The passage behind them collapsed in a cloud of dust and falling rock.

"Move!" Solar shouted, pushing Rowan forward as the ceiling began to give way.

They sprinted through the tunnel, rocks crashing down mere inches behind them. Solar's natural instinct was to burn through the obstruction, but doing so might trigger further collapse. Instead, he focused his remaining energy on speed, practically carrying Rowan as they fled.

They burst into a larger chamber just as the passage sealed itself with rubble. Dust filled the air, causing Rowan to cough violently. Solar created a small energy field around them, filtering the particulates from the air she breathed.

"Thanks," she gasped, leaning against him for support. "But you're getting brighter again."

Solar looked down to see his skin pulsing with golden light, his control slipping as his reserves diminished. "I require solar radiation soon."

"We'll find a way out," Rowan promised, though her expression betrayed doubt.

The chamber they had entered was vast, with a high ceiling that disappeared into darkness. The sound of running water echoed from somewhere ahead. As their eyes adjusted, they could make out strange formations rising from the floor and descending from above. Stalagmites and stalactites, Solar recalled from the Earth educational data packet.

"This is the heart of the system," Rowan whispered, her voice filled with awe despite their predicament. "The Central Chamber."

"You recognize this location?" Solar asked.

"From descriptions. Local guides talk about it. If we're where I think we are, there's a skylight somewhere above us. A natural opening in the ceiling."

Solar immediately looked up, scanning the darkness overhead. If there was an opening, even a small one...

There. A faint, almost imperceptible difference in the quality of darkness above. Without warning, Solar released a controlled pulse of energy, sending a sphere of golden light shooting upward.

The sphere illuminated the chamber in a brief, brilliant flash before striking the ceiling. In that moment of light, they saw the full magnificence of the cave, massive columns of stone, glittering crystal formations, and, crucially, a small circular opening near the highest point of the ceiling.

"There," Solar pointed as darkness returned. "Approximately thirty meters up."

"We can't climb that," Rowan said, her voice tinged with despair. "The walls are too smooth."

Solar assessed their options. His energy was depleting rapidly, but if he could reach that opening, even briefly expose himself to direct sunlight, he could recharge enough to help them both escape.

"I can reach it," he said, his decision made.

"How?" Rowan asked.

Instead of answering, Solar released the restraints on his energy. Golden light exploded outward, illuminating the chamber in a brilliant glow. His physical form began to shift, becoming less solid, more radiant.

"What are you doing?" Rowan shielded her eyes from the sudden brightness.

"Emergency protocol," Solar explained, his voice taking on a resonant quality as his energy expanded. "Temporary conversion to pure energy state. It will allow me to reach the opening."

"And then what?"

"I recharge, return, and we both escape." The plan was logical, though not without risk. In his energy state, he would be vulnerable to Milano's dampening technology if they were nearby. But the alternative was eventual energy depletion and inability to maintain physical form at all.

"Hurry," Rowan urged. "Milano could find us any minute."

Solar nodded, then surrendered to his true nature. His humanoid form dissolved into a column of golden light that shot upward toward the ceiling opening. The sensation was both freedom from physical constraints and, conversely, exposure to detection.

He reached the opening in seconds, passing through the narrow aperture into the blessed radiance of Earth's sun. Even filtered through the atmosphere, the solar radiation was immediate nourishment. Solar's energy signature expanded.

From this vantage point, he could see the canyon stretching before him, the red rock formations glowing in the late-afternoon sun. Milano forces were visible in the distance. The black vehicles sped along on roads, and helicopters circled overhead. But none were in the immediate vicinity of the skylight. For the moment, they remained undetected.

Solar allowed himself exactly ninety seconds of exposure. Then, reluctantly, he withdrew back into the cave, his energy coalescing once more into humanoid form as he descended to where Rowan waited.

"Better?" she asked, noting his brighter, more stable appearance.

"Functional," he confirmed. "But we must find an exit large enough for both of us."

They began exploring the chamber's perimeter, looking for passages that might lead outward rather than deeper into the system. The sound of water grew louder as they approached the far side of the space.

"There," Rowan pointed to where a stream emerged from one wall and disappeared through another. "Water always finds a way out."

They followed the stream, which flowed through a passage just large enough for them to walk single file. Solar led the way, his restored glow providing illumination. The tunnel wound downward for several minutes before gradually beginning to rise again.

"Good sign," Rowan commented. "If it's rising, it might lead to the surface."

Solar remained alert for signs of Milano. His enhanced senses detected no immediate threats, but that could change at any moment. And behind every thought of escape lurked a more personal concern.

Where was Dani?

He had last seen her leaving the Desert Suite with Rowan. Had she gone back there after they fled? Was she captured? Was she searching for him even now?

The tunnel curved sharply, then opened onto a ledge overlooking another chamber. Below them, the stream plunged into a pool before continuing its journey. The drop was significant, at least ten meters to the water below.

"End of the line," Rowan sighed.

Solar assessed the situation. "The water may lead to an exit."

"That looks deeper into the system," Rowan

countered. "And that drop could break bones if we hit wrong. We should backtrack."

Before Solar could respond, he sensed a shift in the darkness.

"We need to keep moving," Rowan urged, her human eyes seeming to be nearly blind in the darkness. She had been relying on Solar's faint glow to navigate the treacherous terrain.

"Agreed." Solar helped her up a particularly steep incline, careful to moderate his temperature. Humans were so fragile, their skin burning at temperatures his people considered comfortable. Not Dani, though. She liked his fire.

They continued in relative silence, Solar scanning constantly for signs of pursuit. Milano's operatives had proven more resourceful than anticipated, their technology approaching Zorveyan capabilities.

"What exactly are these weapons Milano possesses?" Solar asked. The question had been burning in his mind since the attack. The energy dampeners, in particular, suggested an advanced understanding of extraterrestrial physiology.

Rowan's breathing was labored as she climbed. "I don't know. I've ever seen them before."

They emerged into another chamber where the ceiling rose high above them, disappearing into darkness. All of these caves looked the same. Shafts of sunlight penetrated through cracks in the rock, creating spotlights on the cave floor. Solar automatically walked to stand within the light and soaked in what energy he could.

"We're getting closer to the surface," Rowan said.

Before he could answer, Solar felt the darkness shift. He immediately dimmed his light, but it was too late. They'd been spotted.

"Don't move," a familiar voice commanded as Lunar's figure materialized, literally flowing out of the shadows like liquid night.

"Lunar," Solar identified, his tone a mixture of relief and irritation.

Lunar grabbed Rowan by the arm and pulled her away from a deep hole in the cave floor.

Where have you been while we fought for our lives?" Solar asked.

"Observing and preparing an escape route," Lunar replied coolly. He turned his gaze toward Rowan. "Where is Eclipse?"

Solar watched as Rowan flinched at the question.

"He stayed behind," she said, her voice tight, "to hold them off."

Something shifted in Lunar's expression. Concern, perhaps? It was difficult to read emotions on his shadowy features, even for Solar who had known him longer than these humans.

"Milano has deployed energy-dampening technology," Solar explained, his irritation at the situation bleeding into his tone. "They found us at the Desert Suite and attacked in force."

"I am aware," Lunar said. "Poppy and I witnessed their deployment from the canyon rim. She's securing transportation while I tracked your energy signatures to find you." His gaze returned to Rowan. "You left a rather obvious trail."

"I'm sorry I don't have shadow-walking powers," Rowan snapped.

Solar hid his amusement at her defiance. It would seem he was not the only one irritated by Lunar.

Another distant rumble shook the cave, this one weaker than before. Solar's energy pulsed with concern. Each explosion represented Eclipse fighting, or possibly falling prey to, Milano's forces.

"We must keep moving," Lunar urged. "An exit suitable to your dimensions is this way."

He led them through a series of increasingly narrow passages, at times seeming to merge with the shadows completely. Solar followed behind Rowan, providing light for her to navigate the difficult terrain. His mind, however, was increasingly occupied with a single thought.

Dani. Where was Dani?

If Lunar had found Poppy, surely he would know about Dani as well. But Solar hesitated to ask, unwilling to reveal the depth of his concern before Rowan and Lunar. Such emotional attachments were not the way of the Solarus Elite Guard. They were tactical disadvantages, vulnerabilities that could be exploited.

Yet the question burned within him, brighter than his physical form.

"Wait," Rowan gasped as they climbed a particularly steep section. "I need to catch my breath."

"There is no time," Lunar insisted. "Milano's forces are deploying throughout the canyon. They have devices that flash with light when they detect our energy signatures."

"Energy scanners," Rowan mumbled to herself. "Like the ones they used to find us at the retreat."

"Precisely," Lunar confirmed. "We must reach Poppy's vehicle before they establish a perimeter."

Solar helped Rowan up a particularly difficult incline, his mind still divided between immediate survival and concern for Dani. As they ascended, the air grew fresher, the sense of oppressive darkness lifting. They were nearing the surface.

"What about Eclipse?" Rowan insisted again. "We can't just leave him."

"Eclipse is capable of defending himself," Lunar said. "And he would prioritize the mission over his individual safety."

"This isn't a mission anymore," Rowan argued. "This is survival."

"Same objective, different terminology," Solar stated, though he understood her emotional response. Humans formed attachments quickly and invested a kind of meaning in personal connections that his people viewed as secondary to duty.

Yet wasn't that exactly what he was doing with his concern for Dani?

They climbed quietly for a few minutes before reaching a narrow crevice illuminated by natural light filtering from above. Lunar indicated a sequence of handholds etched into the rock face.

"This leads to the surface," he explained. "Poppy will be waiting with transportation approximately half a kilometer north of the exit point."

Solar watched as Rowan began the ascent, her human frailty evident in her trembling limbs and labored breathing. Despite this, she persisted with admirable determination. Solar followed after her, his restored energy making the climb effortless for him. Lunar flowed up last, barely distinguishable from the shadows cast by the rocks.

As they neared the opening, a human hand reached down from above. Poppy's face appeared, her expression a mix of concern and determination.

"Hurry," Poppy urged. "Helicopters are coming back around."

With effort, Rowan pulled herself out of the crevice and onto the sunbaked red rock of the canyon rim. Solar emerged next, his golden form immediately absorbing the sunlight. His energy surged, restoring depleted reserves and strengthening his physical cohesion. Lunar flowed up last, immediately contracting his shadow form to avoid detection in the daylight.

"Where's Eclipse?" Poppy asked.

"Still in the caves," Rowan said, her voice tight. "He stayed behind to fight off Milano."

Poppy's eyes widened. "We need to go back for him. No one gets left behind."

"No time," Lunar said, pointing skyward.

A black helicopter appeared over the canyon ridge, its rotors slicing through the desert air. Below it, dust clouds rose from multiple vehicles traversing the off-road trails.

"They're preparing to flush us out," Lunar observed.

"This way," Poppy urged, leading them toward a cluster of boulders where, improbably, an ancient vehicle with a flimsy top was hidden. Solar frowned at the questionable transportation. What kind of haphazard rescue operation was this?

Solar scanned the area, searching for any sign of Dani. His energy pulsed with increasing anxiety.

"Where is Dani?" he finally asked, unable to contain the question any longer.

No one seemed to hear him as they all climbed into the vehicle. He found himself squished in the back, too close to Lunar for comfort. The jeep's engine sputtered to life like a spaceship on its last takeoff.

"What about Dani?" Rowan asked. "She was supposed to warn you about the attack."

Solar leaned forward to hear the answer.

"We found her in the caves looking for you," Poppy explained, throwing the jeep into gear. "She escaped the retreat in an alien flash mob of all things. She's meeting us at the rendezvous point with supplies."

Relief washed through Solar, causing his light to flare momentarily before he brought it under control. She was safe. The knowledge settled in him like a stabilizing force, allowing him to focus on immediate concerns.

As the jeep bounced along the rugged canyon trail, Solar found the vibrations unpleasant and the entire machine inefficient. His gaze remained fixed on the horizon, searching for any sign of Milano's forces or the rendezvous point where Dani waited. The Earth's sun beat down on his skin, replenishing his depleted energy reserves with each passing moment. He would need his full strength for whatever came next.

The thought of Dani, with her fierce independence, her mastery of fire, and her fearlessness in the face of his alien nature, sparked something unfamiliar within his energy core. These humans had awakened sensations that the Elite Guard training had never prepared him for. Emotions that should have been tactical weaknesses instead felt like sources of power. And if Milano harmed Dani, they would discover just how dangerous a fully charged Solarus warrior could truly be.

11

THE MOTORCYCLE ENGINE ROARED BENEATH Dani as she gunned it over a ridge, momentarily airborne before slamming back to earth. Pain shot through her freshly-wrapped ankle, but she gritted her teeth against it. The makeshift splint she'd created from medical supplies at the animal clinic was holding. Barely.

She'd raided the vet clinic's emergency stores. Painkillers, antibiotics, bandages, burn treatments, everything she could imagine needing for injured aliens on the run. Though, to be honest, she wasn't sure which of the medications could work for humans or aliens. She might have had just supplied Poppy with animal meds. Her backpack full of supplies and alien tech bounced against her spine as she navigated the rough terrain, the damp weight a constant reminder of what was at stake.

A helicopter thundered overhead, black against the deepening sky. Dani immediately swerved off the dirt track, sliding the motorcycle behind a massive red rock formation. She cut the engine, heart pounding as she waited, listening to the rhythmic thump of rotors. The chopper hovered for an agonizing minute before continuing its sweep toward the east.

Too close.

The rendezvous point Poppy had indicated was still five miles across open desert, and daylight was fading. She'd need to push harder if she wanted to reach it before dark, but staying invisible to Milano's air patrols was equally crucial.

She restarted the motorcycle, wincing as her injured ankle protested when she kicked the stand up. The animal clinic stocked painkillers for dogs and cats, not humans, so she had no clue which ones would work for her. She'd been forced to grab over-the-counter pills from the receptionist's desk. They dulled the edge, but not enough.

A glint of metal caught her eye in the distance. A

roadblock had been set up on the main canyon access road. Milano had established checkpoints faster than Poppy had predicted. The direct route was now cut off.

"Guess we're going cross-country," Dani muttered to herself, calculating a new path through the rugged landscape.

She gunned the engine and set off parallel to the road but hidden from it, racing through scrubby vegetation and over rocky terrain that the motorcycle was never designed to handle. Each impact jarred her injured ankle, each jolt a fresh reminder of her recklessness in the cave. But Solar was worth it. Worth every agonizing bump and risky maneuver.

The terrain grew increasingly treacherous as she ventured deeper into the backcountry. Loose rocks scattered beneath the tires, threatening to send her skidding. Twice she nearly wiped out navigating steep inclines. The third time, the back wheel caught on a hidden rock, and the motorcycle fishtailed wildly.

Dani fought for control, leaning hard into the skid. For one heart-stopping moment, the bike tilted dangerously to one side, nearly crushing her injured leg. With a desperate wrench of the handlebars, she managed to right it, but the violent maneuver sent a fresh wave of agony through her ankle.

"Shit," she hissed through clenched teeth, momentarily stopping to catch her breath. The sun was sinking faster now, the rocks catching fire with the last golden rays. The same light that had poured from Solar's skin when he held her.

No time to rest. No time to think about what might have happened to him.

She pushed on, navigating more by instinct. The motorcycle's headlight was too risky to use with Milano's patrols overhead, so she relied on the fading natural light, squinting to make out the path ahead.

As she crested a rise, a flash of movement in her peripheral vision made her heart stutter. Headlights moved fast along a parallel ridge about half a mile away. Not just one vehicle, but three, their powerful spotlights sweeping the terrain.

Milano search teams.

Fuck.

Dani cut her engine immediately and let momentum carry her down the far side of the ridge, out of sight. But she'd miscalculated. The decline was steeper than it appeared, and without power to control her descent, the motorcycle picked up speed rapidly.

The front wheel hit a depression, and Dani felt herself becoming airborne. For one suspended moment, she was flying, and then reality crashed back as she and the motorcycle parted ways. She tumbled through the air, instinctively tucking into a roll as years of martial arts training kicked in.

She hit the ground hard, the impact knocking the wind from her lungs. Pain exploded in her shoulder and side as she rolled uncontrollably down the rocky slope, finally coming to a stop in a cloud of dust.

For several seconds, she lay completely still, fighting to draw breath into stunned lungs. When oxygen finally returned, it brought with it an inventory of fresh injuries. Ribs, bruised, maybe cracked. Left shoulder, definitely wrenched. Right ankle, somehow, miraculously, still contained in its makeshift splint, though throbbing with renewed intensity.

The motorcycle lay on its side twenty feet away, front wheel still spinning lazily. The backpack had torn free during her fall and rested nearby, its contents thankfully still secured inside.

"Get up," she commanded herself. "Move."

The sound of engines grew louder. The Milano team had heard her crash, or worse, spotted her. Either way, they were coming.

Dani forced herself to her feet, biting back a cry as her body protested. She staggered to the motorcycle and heaved it upright, ignoring the screaming pain in her shoulder. The frame was dented, the left mirror gone, but the engine still caught when she hit the starter.

The headlights on the ridge were closer now, starting to descend her way. She had maybe two minutes before they reached her position.

There was no way to outrun them on the damaged bike, not with her injuries. She needed a diversion.

Dani reached for the backpack, frantically searching through the medical supplies until her fingers closed around what she needed. A bottle of alcohol. Surgical grade, nearly pure ethanol. She tore a strip from her already-ripped shirt and stuffed it into the bottle's mouth, creating a crude wick.

Fire. Her oldest friend. Her most reliable weapon.

The lights were closing in, now just a quarter of a mile away and gaining quickly. Dani gunned the motorcycle's engine, fighting to maintain control with one hand while holding her makeshift explosive. She sped parallel to the approaching vehicles, leading them away from the rendezvous point.

When she'd put enough distance between herself and her intended path, she pulled the lighter from her pocket. It was the same one that had survived the cave. With a practiced flick, she lit the wick and hurled the bottle toward a patch of dry brush.

The explosion was more impressive than she'd expected. Flames erupted instantly, racing through the parched vegetation. The Milano vehicles skidded to a halt as a wall of fire spread between them and Dani.

She didn't wait to see if they'd find a way around. With the last of her strength, she wrenched the motorcycle around and sped off in the direction of the rendezvous point, the growing darkness swallowing her as the fire blazed behind.

The final miles were a blur of pain and determination. Twice she nearly blacked out, forcing herself to stay conscious through sheer willpower. The bike's engine began to stutter. She didn't know if it was damaged in the crash or running out of fuel. Either way, it wouldn't last much longer.

"Please, please, please," she begged the bike. "Just a little closer."

The motorcycle gave a final, protesting cough as she guided it into the canyon entrance, then died completely. Dani half-rode, half-wobbled the last few yards before the bike tipped sideways, depositing her roughly on the ground.

She lay on the desert floor, panting heavily and fighting the waves of pain washing over her. Dani didn't think she could stand up even if she tried. Every muscle screamed in protest, and every breath sent sharp pains through her ribs. Tears spilled hot over her cheeks. Her body couldn't take much more.

But worse than the physical pain was the fear eating away at her core.

Where was Solar? Was he still alive? Still fighting? Or had Milano's mercenaries subdued him? Taken him to some secret facility to be studied and dissected?

Fear took her imagination to some dark places.

"Solar," she whispered in determination. "I'm coming."

The thought sent a surge of renewed energy through her exhausted body. She hadn't survived a cave collapse, a motorcycle crash, and a Milano pursuit just to give up now. Solar was alive. He had to be. Milano would not win.

And until she saw him again, felt his impossible warmth, witnessed that golden glow that seemed to reach inside her very soul, she would keep fighting. Keep surviving. Because somehow, in just a few days, this alien had become something precious to her. Something worth burning for.

Dani straightened and pushed to her feet despite the pain. She limped across the uneven terrain. Her gaze stayed fixed on the dark canyon entrance. Waiting. Watching. Ready.

12

THE JEEP BOUNCED VIOLENTLY AS IT NAVIGATED a particularly rough section of the canyon floor. Solar maintained his position in the back seat through sheer will, his energy anchoring him in place while Lunar seemed to flow with the motion, his shadow form adapting to each jarring impact. The silver emergency blanket Poppy had thrown over them to mask their energy signatures crinkled with each movement, creating an irritating sound that Solar's enhanced hearing found particularly grating. It also uncomfortably trapped Lunar's energy next to his.

His mind, however, was focused on a single objective. Find Dani.

"There," Lunar said suddenly, pointing ahead.

Solar's energy surged at the sight of a figure

standing in the desert, waving urgently. Even from this distance, he recognized the distinctive red of her hair, the determined set of her shoulders. Dani.

Relief flooded his system with such intensity that his skin brightened involuntarily beneath the concealing blanket. Lunar grunted at the release of his energy. Solar didn't care. She was alive. She was here. That was all that mattered.

Poppy pulled up beside her, and Dani immediately climbed in, squeezing into the back between Solar and Lunar. The moment she settled beside him, Solar felt her warmth, sensed the subtle electromagnetic signature that was uniquely hers. Something within his core energy aligned in response, a synchronization that felt both foreign and essential.

"Thank god you made it," she said breathlessly. "Milano teams are swarming everywhere." She looked around, her eyes scanning their faces. "Where's Eclipse?"

Solar noticed how she winced slightly as she shifted position and the careful way she held herself. She was injured. The realization sent a protective surge through his energy field that he struggled to contain. Who had hurt her? How severely?

The question about Eclipse hung in the air, unanswered but for a slight shake of Poppy's head.

"We need to keep moving," Lunar said after a moment. "Milano will expand their search perimeter once they realize we've escaped the caves."

Poppy nodded and sped up, following a wash until it merged with a more defined trail. Solar maintained a careful distance from Dani despite the cramped quarters, aware that his energy emissions might harm her if not properly controlled. Yet even this minimal proximity brought a strange comfort.

"I've got water, food, and some basic first aid in my pack," Dani offered, passing a water bottle to Rowan. "And we managed to grab these from the suite."

She pulled out a small object that Solar recognized immediately as Eclipse's energy stone, along with several other Zorveyan devices. His surprise must have shown on his face.

"How did you know to take these?" he asked.

"I figured they might be important," Dani explained. "When Milano started closing in, one of Rowan's alien enthusiast friends figured they shouldn't get their hands on any more alien tech. They gave it to me for safekeeping."

Her simple explanation bore none of the self-congratulations a Solarus warrior might have displayed after such a mission.

Rowan eagerly reached for the stone. "Can we use this to contact him?"

"Possibly," Solar told her. "The energy stones are attuned to their owners. It might respond to Eclipse's signature if he's within range."

As Rowan examined Eclipse's energy stone, Solar's attention remained fixed on Dani. He felt her leg slide against his. In the fading light, he could see scrapes along her arms, a darkening bruise on her cheek, and the careful way she kept adjusting on the seat whenever they hit a rough patch of desert. What had she gone through to get back to them?

Why would she put herself through it? For him? The concept was as foreign as it was compelling.

The jeep jostled over rutted earth, causing Dani to wince visibly. Solar instinctively reached out, his hand stopping just short of touching her shoulder.

"You're injured," he whispered, his voice low enough that only she could hear.

Dani met his gaze, a small, pained smile touching her lips. "I've had worse."

"How did this happen?" The question emerged more forcefully than he'd intended.

"Motorcycle crash," she admitted. "Milano patrols came. I had to go off-road."

Solar processed this information, his energy

surging with a complex mixture of concern and admiration. "You should not have taken such risks."

"Says the alien who got hunted through a cave system by mercenaries," Dani countered, her green eyes holding his with a defiance that somehow made his core energy resonate more strongly.

"You set a fire to escape?" Solar observed, detecting the faint scent of smoke and accelerant still clinging to her clothing.

"As a diversion." Her eyes widened slightly. "How did you—?"

"Your scent carries traces of combustion patterns consistent with accelerants. And there is residue on your fingers indicating direct contact with a flame source."

A genuine smile spread across her face despite her obvious discomfort. "That's either really creepy or really hot. I haven't decided which."

Solar was uncertain how to respond to this statement. Creepy was clearly negative, while hot suggested his temperature was pleasing, though humans typically used this term metaphorically rather than literally.

"I am hot," he finally answered.

"And very literal," she teased.

Before he could formulate a response, the jeep

hit another bump, causing Dani to pitch forward. Solar moved instinctively, his arm wrapping around her to stabilize her position. The contact sent a surge of energy between them, a harmonic resonance that momentarily brightened his golden skin beneath the concealing blanket.

"Sorry," Dani murmured, though she made no immediate move to pull away from his supporting arm.

"No apology is necessary," Solar replied, equally reluctant to break contact. "Your energy signature remains compatible with mine."

She chuckled. "You say the cutest things."

"I do not believe I am cute. Rather, I am manly." He tapped his implant. "Perhaps my translator is broken."

"Actually, can I borrow your heat?" Dani reached for his hand and pulled it to her shoulder. She sighed and closed her eyes. "Better than a heating pad."

The jeep continued its jarring journey across the backcountry, gradually leaving the more traveled areas behind. The terrain became increasingly rugged, the trail sometimes disappearing entirely before reappearing hundreds of yards later.

"How much further?" Solar asked, his form flickering slightly with each major bump. The constant dampening of his energy to avoid detection was taking its toll, and he could feel Dani's body temperature dropping beside him as night settled over the desert.

"About five more miles," Poppy answered from the driver's seat. "We'll be there before full dark."

As they bounced onward, deeper into the wilderness, the conversation turned to Milano and their technology. Solar contributed his tactical assessment, but his attention remained primarily on Dani. Her injuries required treatment, yet she showed no sign of yielding to pain or fatigue. Her resilience was remarkable for a species with such physical limitations.

"This is my fault," Rowan said quietly. "We should never have left the suite."

"No," Solar countered her illogical statement. "Milano was already tracking us. They would have found us regardless."

"Solar is correct," Lunar added. "Their technology is advanced. They were hunting us systematically."

"Which brings us back to how they got that technology in the first place," Dani said. "I mean, energy weapons specifically designed to counter alien powers? That's not something they developed overnight."

"The missing Milano founder," Rowan said. "Darren reminded me of the rumors that Milano's founder disappeared after claiming aliens had abducted him."

"Perhaps not a claim," Lunar mused. "Perhaps fact."

The sunlight faded rapidly, casting the rocks in deepening shades of crimson and purple. Twilight approached. Eclipse's time. Solar felt Dani shiver slightly beside him and adjusted his energy emissions to provide more full-body warmth without risking detection.

"Thank you," she whispered, leaning closer.

A distant sound caught Solar's attention. The high-pitched whine did not sound like Milano's helicopters. Something smaller, faster, approached rapidly from the east.

"Incoming aerial vehicle," he warned, straightening to scan the darkening sky.

Lunar tensed beside them, his shadow form contracting to its most condensed state. "Not Milano's pattern."

"What do I do?" Poppy yelled over the noise.

The whine grew louder, and a flickering light appeared over the ridge to their right, moving erratically as if the pilot had limited control of the craft.

"Get off the trail," Solar instructed sharply. "Find cover."

Poppy immediately complied, steering the jeep behind a cluster of large boulders. They moved along in tense silence as the sound grew closer, the light bobbing and weaving as it approached.

"That flight pattern seems familiar," Lunar observed, a note of disbelief in his cold voice.

As the craft cleared the ridge, Solar's energy flared with recognition and dismay. The small transport pod was unmistakably of Galaxy Brides' design, though it appeared to have been repaired with Earth materials, including what looked like duct tape covering multiple hull breaches.

"No," Solar groaned. "Not them."

"Slow down," Rowan ordered.

"Who?" Dani asked, squinting at the approaching craft.

"Bob and Gary," Solar replied.

"Bob, Gary, and Pudding," Lunar said at the same time.

The pod wobbled dangerously as it descended

toward their position, its landing struts deploying unevenly. It touched down twenty meters from their hiding place, a cloud of dust enveloping it as the engines sputtered before cutting out entirely.

Poppy slowed the car as they approached the ship. "It's too soon. We had more time."

A hatch opened on the side, and a familiar yellow face peered out, wearing an expression of forced cheerfulness. "Hello! Yoo-hoo! We've come to rescue you!"

"They're going to get us all killed," Solar muttered, watching as Gary clambered awkwardly from the craft, followed by Bob's smaller form. They didn't get out of the vehicle.

"Are those your alien matchmakers?" Dani asked.

"Unfortunately," Solar confirmed.

Gary waved enthusiastically, as if they were meeting at a social gathering rather than hiding from a ruthless corporate security force. "There you are. We saw the fire signal and came as quickly as we could!"

"Fire signal?" Dani whispered.

"Your diversion," Solar explained. "They must have mistaken it for a deliberate communication."

Gary and Bob hurried toward them, both wearing what appeared to be hastily modified skin-suits that made them look like particularly unattractive Earth children with oversized heads.

"We've been searching everywhere for you," Gary announced as they reached the jeep. "The extraction coordinates have been compromised. Milano has the entire area under surveillance." He peered into the vehicle, counting occupants. "Oh dear. We weren't expecting so many of you."

"The extraction is still proceeding?" Solar demanded.

"Of course," Bob interjected, speaking for the first time. "Just relocated. And accelerated. As in, right now. Our window is closing rapidly."

"Weren't there three of you?" Gary frowned.

"We can't find Eclipse," Rowan said. "Can you track him?"

"Eclipse, that's right," Gary said.

"Ignore him. He bumped his foot," Bob slapped a hand in the general direction of Gary's mouth.

"Your pod cannot accommodate all of us," Lunar observed.

"Well, no," Gary admitted, tugging nervously at his skin-suit. "It's really only designed for three passengers plus pilot. Four if everyone breathes in shifts."

"Then it's useless to us," Rowan stated firmly. "We're not leaving anyone behind."

"Actually," Bob said, his expression turning surprisingly serious, "Milano's forces are converging on this location as we speak. They might have detected our landing."

"What?" Poppy hissed. "You led them straight to us?"

"Not intentionally," Gary protested. "But our stealth systems were, shall we say, somewhat compromised by the emergency repairs."

Solar processed this new information. "How long until they reach us?"

"Twenty Earth minutes, perhaps less," Bob replied. "They're mobilizing from multiple directions."

"We need to split up," Lunar stated, his tactical assessment aligning with Solar's own. "Increase survival probability through diversification of targets."

"Precisely what we were thinking," Gary exclaimed, too loudly for their precarious situation. "Inverse targets."

"No," Rowan denied immediately. "We stay together until we find Eclipse."

"The pod can transport the two of you to the new extraction coordinates," Bob said. "The humans can continue by ground as decoys."

"Eclipse can take care of himself," Lunar stated in a poor attempt to comfort Rowan.

"The cabin I was telling you about is still the safest immediate option," Poppy insisted. "We should all go there and regroup."

"But you are already grouped," Gary said. "We need you to ungroup."

"The others can continue to the cabin location in the Earth vehicle, where we can arrange secondary extraction once the heat is off," Bob persisted, directing his attention at Solar and Lunar. He gave a small wave for them to follow.

Solar exchanged a glance with Lunar, and a rare moment of perfect understanding passed between them. Tactically, the Galaxy Brides representatives were correct, despite their general incompetence. Splitting up would increase the overall chances of mission success, even if it increased the risk to the three women.

"Solar and Dani should go with them," Lunar said, surprising everyone. "Solar's energy signature is the most detectable, especially now as we face darkness. He is the most likely to draw Milano to all of us. And Dani requires medical attention that the extraction vessel can provide."

"What? No," Dani protested. "My ankle is fine. We're not leaving you guys to face Milano alone."

"It's strategically sound," Solar said quietly, though the prospect of separating from the group troubled him more than he would have expected. "Milano developed specific countermeasures for our energy signatures. If Lunar and I remain together, the capture probability increases substantially."

Dani looked at him in protest. "But—"

A distant rumble interrupted her, followed by the distinctive thump of helicopter rotors.

"Decision time," Gary urged, his yellow skin paling noticeably. "Milano's air support is incoming."

Solar decided for them. "Dani and I will go with you. Lunar, protect them." He nodded toward Rowan and Poppy. "We will search for Eclipse from the sky, and we will rendezvous at the secondary extraction point once it's secured."

"Wait," Dani began, but Solar had already moved, lifting her carefully from the jeep despite her protests. "We can't go into... We can't fly... I mean, up there?"

Dani looked up at the sky and trembled. She shook her head.

"Perfectly safe," Gary said.

"Your injuries require treatment," he said firmly, not putting her down as he held her in his arms. "And I can better protect you in a smaller group."

She looked up again at the sky. "That's not—"

"No time to argue," Gary interrupted, already hurrying back toward the pod. "Those helicopters will be on us in minutes."

"Do you want me to put her to sleep?" Bob offered Solar. "It would be the kind thing to do."

"No!" Dani protested, leaning into Solar's chest. "Don't you touch me."

Solar carried Dani toward the pod. She clutched her backpack of supplies to her chest. He set her down gently at the pod's entrance.

"We will see them again," he assured her, though he had no tactical basis for such certainty.

Dani looked back at the jeep, where Poppy was already restarting the engine. "This feels wrong."

"I know," Solar agreed. "But it is necessary."

"I don't think I can do this," she whispered, looking up to the sky. "I mean, this is a spaceship. They crashed the last one you were in."

"That was Harris," Gary yelled. "Come on then."

Solar urged her into the pod, finding the interior even more cramped than its external appearance suggested. Gary took the pilot's seat, while Bob squeezed in beside him at what passed for a control panel. Solar and Dani were left with a space barely large enough for one adult human, let alone an alien warrior and his injured companion. Their estimate of being able to fit Lunar and Eclipse in here with Solar at the same time only worked if they were willing to comingle their essences for the duration of the flight.

Gross. He didn't want his essence floating inside the other two.

"Um, you might want to hold onto something," Gary advised as he initiated the launch sequence. "The stabilizers are a bit theoretical at this point."

"Where are the straps?" Solar demanded.

"Also theoretical," Gary said.

Solar positioned himself to brace Dani against the inevitable turbulence, his arm encircling her protectively as the pod's engines whined to life. She trembled, and he felt the shift in her energy as it flowed into him. In return, he tried to give her his calm. It worked. Her shaking subsided.

Through the small viewport, he watched as the jeep sped away, vanishing into the darkness of the canyon. The helicopters were visible now, their searchlights sweeping the terrain as they approached.

The pod lurched upward, then sideways, then into a spin that caused warning lights to flash across the control panel. Gary and Bob shouted technical jargon at each other that Solar strongly suspected they didn't actually understand.

"Compensating for rotational torque," Gary called out.

"That's not what rotational torque means," Bob shouted back.

"Well, whatever it is, I'm compensating for it!"

Dani closed her eyes tightly and gripped him. Her breathing became labored. The frantic beat of her heart drummed in his ears.

The pod stabilized momentarily before dipping toward the ground, then shooting upward so rapidly that Solar had to brace himself and Dani against the ceiling.

"Sorry," Gary called cheerfully. "Still getting used to the Earth's atmosphere. Very thick."

"Is it too late to go back to the Milano agents?" Dani muttered against Solar's chest. She pressed her hand against her mouth and closed her eyes tightly.

Despite the dangerous absurdity of their situation, Solar felt his energy responding to her proximity. Her nearness made him feel braver. She remained pressed against him during their chaotic ascent. Something had changed between them in the short time they'd known each other. It was profound and unexpected.

When the time came, he didn't think he'd be able to let her go.

The pod finally achieved a somewhat stable flight path, climbing above the canyon walls and accelerating eastward. Below them, the helicopter searchlights converged on their launch point, finding nothing but disturbed dust and tire tracks leading in the opposite direction.

"See? Flawless escape!" Gary declared, as a panel beside him sparked and fell off entirely. "Now, who's hungry? I've packed Earth snacks. Very authentic. We have cheese dust cylinders and sugar discs."

Dani looked up at Solar, her expression caught between disbelief and reluctant amusement. "Are we sure this is better than the cave full of Milano agents?"

"That remains to be determined," Solar replied honestly. "But I find I prefer facing either threat with you by my side."

Her smile in response was like a sunrise after the darkness of the cave. Whatever dangers awaited them, whatever absurdities they would endure with Bob and Gary as their pilots, Solar knew with a certainty that transcended strategic analysis that he was precisely where he needed to be.

Dani's eyes turned to the viewing screen as they watched the ground disappearing below. He felt her soft breath against his skin as she whispered, "Fuck me. I'm in outer space."

13

Dani had never considered what outer space would smell like. If someone had asked, she might have guessed nothing. Space was a vacuum, an emptiness, and she would assume had an absence of scent. But as Galaxy Brides' battered transport pod broke through Earth's atmosphere, she discovered space smelled exactly like burning electrical components and Gary's pungent cologne.

"Is it supposed to be making that noise?" she asked, gripping Solar's arm as the entire vessel shuddered violently. She felt him radiating a consistent calm, and it helped her from completely losing her shit.

"Absolutely!" Gary called cheerfully from the

pilot's seat. "That's just the atmospheric transfer protocols adjusting to your planet's unusual density."

"He's lying," Solar said. "Nothing is supposed to make that noise."

They were in outer space.

Outer fucking space.

Nausea churned in her stomach, and she pressed her hand to her mouth as if the symbolic gesture could keep her from throwing up.

The pod's interior was barely larger than a truck bed, packed with mismatched equipment covered in blinking lights. What she found most concerning was the steady increase in red lights replacing green ones. Sure, she couldn't prove that red meant bad on an alien ship, but it didn't feel like a good thing.

Another violent shudder ran through the ship. Dani's stomach lurched as the artificial gravity flickered, momentarily lifting her a few inches before slamming her back down. Pain shot through her injured ankle and ribs.

Solar's arm tightened protectively around her.

"Your technology is inadequate," he stated, glaring at the back of Gary's oversized head. "This vessel's integrity is compromised in seventeen different places."

"Eighteen now," Bob corrected as a panel above

them detached completely, exposing a tangle of wires that sparked ominously. "But who's counting?"

Dani closed her eyes, trying to control her lurching stomach. This was not how she wanted to die. The ship pitched again, sending her shoulder crashing into a protruding console. She bit back a cry of pain. Tears rolled down her face, and she tried to draw her legs to her chest. Solar kept hold of her the best he could.

"She requires medical attention," Solar insisted, his golden light intensifying with concern. "You claimed your vessel had treatment capabilities."

"It does! It does!" Gary spun his chair around, apparently unconcerned that no one was piloting the ship. "We'll take her to the medical bay just as soon as I find where we docked our ship. At least we know it's cloaking works, right?"

"Your controls are smoking," Solar stated.

"Not to worry." Gary slapped his hand on the metal console. "We have a quaternary system."

"We do?" Bob asked, genuinely surprised.

"Well, we will once you install it," Gary replied cheerfully.

Bob nodded as if that was helpful information.

The ship began to spin in fast circles, and the viewing screen made her dizzy. Gary panicked and turned back around to fly. Dani leaned her head against Solar's shoulder.

"Slow it down," Bob ordered.

They lurched as if someone slammed on the brakes, jerking violently. Dani gripped Solar tighter. It became hard to breathe, and she felt as if she might pass out. A loud *thunk* sounded, jarring the pod. The hull vibrated as a grotesque scraping noise scratched along the metal exterior.

"There it is," Gary exclaimed. "Right where we left it. And you were worried we wouldn't find it."

The ship walls groaned, and Dani saw a hatch opening to let them off.

"All right, good friends, let's move along," Bob said. The air hissed violently and blue light streamed into their darker pod. "Quickly. Quickly. Plenty of oxygen on the mothership."

Solar swept her up into his arms, and she held on tight as he walked her through the hatch onto a much larger vessel.

"The medical bay is right through that door." Gary pointed to a narrow door halfway down a corridor.

"Don't be scared," Bob explained, as if that clarified anything. "Completely safe for most humanoids. Very exclusive technology. Very rarely any probing."

Bob made a strange wheezing noise, and she wasn't sure if he lacked air or was laughing.

Solar set Dani on her feet, supporting most of her weight as she hobbled toward the supposed medical bay. Her entire body ached from the motorcycle crash, the cave adventure, and now their violent ascent into space. She didn't have high hopes for whatever passed as Galaxy Brides' first aid.

The door slid open, revealing a space that was much larger than the pod they had just left. Equipment that appeared to be salvaged from half a dozen different alien technologies lined the walls. A soft blue light illuminated a central examination table.

"What is all this?" Dani whispered, momentarily forgetting her pain. "It doesn't look safe. Or sterile."

"It is an older model but standard medical technology," Solar explained, guiding her toward the table.

Dani swallowed hard and gave a nervous laugh. "I don't suppose they can just drop me off at an Earth doctor? Or abduct one."

"We cannot risk them flying back. Not now. It's too dangerous. Lie down," Solar instructed, his golden eyes scanning the various instruments. "This is much like the standard medical array on my planet, though adapted with questionable modifications."

Dani eased herself onto the table, wincing as her ribs protested. "How bad is it going to hurt?"

Solar's expression softened. "It will not hurt. Most alien cultures do not employ primitive pain-based healing techniques."

Before she could respond, he pressed a sequence of symbols on a panel beside the table. A beam of soft golden light extended from a device overhead, scanning slowly down her body.

Warmth spread through her limbs, not unlike the feeling of Solar's energy when he touched her. The pain in her ankle began to fade, replaced by a pleasant tingling sensation. Lasers concentrated on her stomach, and her ribs stopped aching. Even the scrapes and bruises that covered her arms seemed to be healing before her eyes.

"Holy shit," Dani breathed. "This is amazing."

Solar nodded, studying a display that showed a three-dimensional image of her skeletal structure. "The fracture in your ankle is responding well. Your cracked ribs are being repaired. There is a chip in the bone that lodged near your heart. A wrong impact would have caused great damage to your life. Don't move. It is being repaired."

"So I'll live?" Dani attempted humor, though the reality of their situation was beginning to sink in. She was on an alien spaceship, leaving Earth behind and leaving Poppy, Rowan, and Lunar to face Milano without them. And who knew where Eclipse was. She hoped he was safe.

"Your injuries are healing at an accelerated rate," Solar confirmed, missing her attempt at levity. "Though the equipment's efficiency is compromised by Bob and Gary's modifications."

The ship lurched again, sending several loose instruments crashing to the floor. The healing beam flickered but held steady.

The laser moved to her hip and concentrated on it. "I don't hurt there."

"An ovarian cyst," Solar said. "It has been remedied."

Dani didn't want to discuss her ovaries. A beep sounded.

"Do you require products for your bleeding cycle?" Solar asked.

"You mean my period?" Dani snorted. She hadn't thought of that. Great, period cramps on an alien ship. "Any chance that device can make me skip it this month?"

She was joking, but Solar nodded seriously and touched the panel. The lasers focused on her stomach. "It is done. The lining has been removed for this cycle."

She really didn't want to discuss her lining, either.

Then a thought hit her. Dani tried to sit up, but he turned to look at her, and the intensity of it kept her on the table.

"I haven't taken my birth control pills," she said. "I'm not going to get pregnant, am I? I mean, can I? Can we even?"

"Technically, yes, I can infuse our energies to create a new entity inside of you for gestation, but I do not think this week is an optimal time to carry an offspring," he answered.

Week?

"Yeah, okay, let's not do that," she answered.

"Agreed. Though perhaps at a later time." Solar continued to study the panel.

The ship creaked and vibrated.

"Are we even going to make it to wherever we're going?" Dani asked. She hadn't seriously considered traveling away from Earth. This all happened so fast. "What is your planet called? Zorveya?"

"Zorveya is too far away. We can't abandon the others. We will remain in orbit until we can retrieve them," Solar supplied. "And the probability is..." He paused, his expression darkening. "Lower than I would prefer."

"Great," Dani muttered. "I survive Milano agents, cave collapses, and a motorcycle crash only to die in a malfunctioning alien matchmaking van."

Solar's hand found hers, his touch warm and reassuring. "I will not allow that to happen."

Something in his voice made her believe him. She watched him as he studied her skeleton. Despite everything, despite the absurdity of their situation and the danger they still faced, Dani felt safe with him. Which was ridiculous. They'd known each other for what? Less than a week? And yet there was something between them that transcended time. A connection that felt both terrifying and inevitable.

The healing beam completed its cycle and retracted into the ceiling. Dani sat up cautiously, testing her ankle. The pain was gone, replaced by a mild stiffness.

"Better?" Solar asked.

"Much." She flexed her foot, marveling at the technology that had healed in minutes what would have taken weeks on Earth. "So what now? We just hang out here until they fix their pod?"

Solar's expression turned grim. "That pod is not safe. During our Earth safety training, we had discussed plans to use dimensional fold technology. The extraction devices placed on the planet's surface would create a temporary bridge between spatial coordinates. I believe the best Earth word is wormhole. Though these bridges are temporary and not as stable."

"Attention passengers," Gary's voice echoed through an intercom. "We're preparing for a hyperspace jump in approximately three minutes. Please secure all loose items, bodily appendages, and dimensional anomalies."

Solar helped Dani off the table just as the lights flickered. One of the walls began to flash, revealing a swirling vortex of colors that hurt her eyes to look at directly.

"What the hell is that?" she gasped as Solar pulled her toward the door.

"Interdimensional breach," he explained tersely. "Not lethal, but extremely disorienting if you're caught in it."

The door to the corridor slid open, and Solar practically pushed Dani through it. The medical bay behind them began to warp, the equipment stretching and contracting in impossible ways.

"Minor technical difficulties in the auxiliary medical unit," Bob announced as Solar sealed the door behind them. "Nothing to worry about unless you're still in there."

"Nothing to worry about?" Dani echoed incredulously. "That room literally folded in on itself!"

Their alien hosts were nowhere to be seen. She might as well have been shouting into a vortex.

"Hold on to me," Solar ordered. He pressed his body against hers like a shield and forced her back against the wall as he grabbed hold of a rail.

"What's happening?" She wrapped her arms around his waist. The air felt charged with electricity, and a loud buzzing noise filled her ears.

"This is the safest position," he said, his voice low. "My energy can stabilize against spatial distortion."

Under different circumstances, Dani might have made a joke about his safest position comment, but the increasing vibrations throughout the ship kept her focused on more immediate concerns.

"Hyperjump in ten," Gary's voice announced excitedly. "Nine. Eight..."

"Is this going to hurt?" Dani whispered, pressing closer to Solar's warmth.

"Seven. Six."

"Not if it's executed correctly," Solar answered honestly.

"Five. Four."

"And what are the odds of that?" She clutched Solar's tighter, bracing herself.

"Three."

Solar hesitated. "With Bob and Gary piloting—"

The universe exploded.

At least that's the only way Dani could think to describe what happened. One moment she was braced against a wall in a rickety spaceship, and the next she was everywhere and nowhere all at once. Brilliant colors rushed past her vision. Her body seemed to stretch infinitely while simultaneously compressing to the size of an atom. She tried to scream, but the sound had no meaning in this place.

The only constant was Solar's warmth surrounding her, his energy creating a protective cocoon against the impossible forces tearing at her consciousness. She clung to that sensation, focusing on it with everything she had.

Then, as suddenly as it began, it ended. Reality snapped back into place with brutal force. Dani gasped, drawing in air that tasted metallic and strange. Her heart beat so hard and fast she thought it might choke her.

"Was that normal?" she croaked, her voice sounding wrong in her own ears.

"Not remotely," Solar replied, his arms still tight around her. "But we survived."

Dani didn't like the sound of that.

"Perfect execution. Textbook hyperjump," Gary lied. "We are safely out of detection range. Feel free to roam the ship. There is a delightful rivet pattern in the engine room."

"If the textbook was written by a malfunctioning waste disposal unit," Solar yelled, though Dani wasn't sure if the alien pilots could hear him.

"You should not have told them that we're safe," Bob's voice stated. "We can't guarantee that. It depends on whether we encounter any space-time anomalies. Or Milano pursuit vessels. Or if the dimensional stabilizers give out completely."

"Did you want them to know that?" Gary asked.

"Did you leave the com—" Bob's voice instantly cut off.

Dani slumped against Solar, the reality of their situation terrifying her. Trapped in this rickety ship with Bob and Gary, floating around Earth with possibly no way of knowing what was happening to their friends.

"Seriously, this isn't right. What have we done?" she whispered. "We left them behind."

Solar's hand moved to her face, turning it gently

toward him. His golden eyes held hers, steady and certain. "You needed medical attention. We are lucky we caught the bone shard before it did damage. We survived. And we will continue to survive."

"But the others—"

"Lunar is resourceful," Solar stated. "More capable than I have previously acknowledged. And your Earth friends have demonstrated remarkable adaptability. They will find a way to survive as well."

Dani wanted to believe him. Had to believe him. The alternative was too painful to consider.

"So what now?" she asked.

Solar glanced around the corridor.

"Now we adapt," he said simply. "You learn to navigate this vessel, and we develop a strategy to return to Earth with proper resources."

"Return to Earth?" Dani hadn't dared to hope that was an option.

Solar's expression softened slightly, his golden light pulsing in a way she'd come to recognize as affection. "Did you believe I would abandon your planet permanently? Leave Lunar without reinforcements? Allow Milano to continue their operations unchecked?"

"I didn't know what to think," Dani admitted. "Everything's happened so fast."

"The mission parameters have changed," Solar acknowledged. "But the core objective remains valid. Peace between different species. Connection across boundaries." His hand covered hers. "I have found such a connection. I will not relinquish it."

Before Dani could respond, a loud bang echoed through the ship, followed by a shower of sparks from an overhead panel.

"Minor propulsion fluctuation," Gary announced. "Nothing to worry about."

"That was the secondary stabilizer," Bob contradicted. "We're now running on the tertiary system, which is—did you turn the com device on again? Give me—"

The voices stopped.

Solar sighed, the sound so human it almost made Dani laugh despite their predicament.

"First priority," he said, "I check the security of this vessel. Then we settle into our quarters and find you food."

Dani watched as Solar moved toward a wall and opened up control panels, his warrior's training evident in how quickly he assessed the systems, identified weaknesses, and began implementing solutions. His golden light seemed to strengthen the ship itself, stabilizing fluctuations wherever he touched.

Trapped in a failing spaceship with Bob and Gary. It should have terrified her. And part of her *was* terrified. But watching Solar take command, seeing the certainty with which he faced their situation, Dani felt something else beneath the fear.

Hope.

Not just for their survival, but for what might come after. For the possibility of returning to Earth, of reuniting with their friends, of continuing whatever this was between them that had ignited so quickly and burned so bright.

Dani rolled up her sleeves and moved to Solar's side. "Tell me what to do."

He glanced at her, surprise briefly crossing his features before being replaced by approval. "Can you read this energy distribution matrix?"

The display showed patterns and symbols she'd never seen before. "Not even slightly."

"Then I will teach you," Solar said. "Starting with the basics of subspace navigation and dimensional stabilization."

"Of course," Dani nodded, as if this were a perfectly normal educational opportunity and not a crash course in alien technology while hurtling through interstellar space in a ship held together with the equivalent of alien duct tape. "Let's start with why this panel is smoking."

Solar's lips twitched in what might have been the beginning of a smile. "That would be the tertiary life support system."

"The what now?"

Dani looked at Solar, who merely raised an eyebrow in response.

"Let's fix that first," she suggested. "And then maybe you can teach me how to say 'you're a fucking idiot' in Bob and Gary's language. I have a feeling I'm going to need it."

Solar's expression softened. "That is a phrase I have had frequent cause to employ since meeting them. Don't worry, their translators are working. They will understand you."

As they worked together to stabilize the life support system, Dani realized something important. Yes, they had left Earth behind and were floating in deep space where very few humans had ever been, but she didn't need to be afraid. Not really.

Because for the first time in her life, she wasn't running away from something.

She was running toward someone.

14

Solar had never known darkness like this.

Even in the deepest reaches of space between stars, radiation bathed the universe in a constant glow that his enhanced perception could detect. But this manufactured vessel with its failing systems and questionable construction created a darkness that felt almost personal in its oppression. He wasn't sure how, but it was worse than when they had traveled to Earth.

He stood in what Bob had grandly called the observatory, though it appeared to be nothing more than a storage compartment with a single viewport. Outside, Earth hung suspended against the blackness, a swirl of blue and white that seemed impossibly fragile from this distance. It was strange to watch a planet not in a tidal lock. The light moved across the surface, ever changing it.

Solar pressed his palm against the transparent barrier, allowing his natural radiance to brighten enough to illuminate the cramped space. The golden light revealed walls lined with mismatched storage containers, many of which were labeled with symbols he recognized from half a dozen different star systems. Galaxy Brides' sourcing methods were evidently as questionable as their ethics.

"I thought I'd find you here," Dani's voice came from behind him.

Solar turned to see her silhouetted in the doorway, her form outlined by the dim emergency lighting from the corridor. Even in the near-darkness, she moved with the same precise grace he'd observed during her fire dance. An efficiency of motion that spoke of discipline and control.

"This is the closest I can get to an energy source to rejuvenate myself. And the view helps me calculate," Solar explained, gesturing toward Earth. "I can determine our orbital position and monitor for Milano activity."

Dani moved to stand beside him, close enough that he could sense the subtle electrical currents of her nervous system. The medical treatment had healed her physical injuries, but he detected lingering stress patterns in her biorhythms.

"Any sign of them?" she asked.

"Nothing conclusive. Earth's orbital monitoring systems are primitive but extensive. Milano would require significant resources to launch any pursuit craft without detection." He studied her profile as she gazed at her homeworld. "How are your injuries?"

"Good as new," Dani replied, rotating her previously injured ankle. "Whatever that laser beam was, it works miracles. I've never felt better."

Solar nodded, satisfied with her recovery. "The medical technology prioritizes complete cellular restoration. Your Earth medicine often merely encourages natural healing processes and pharmaceuticals."

"How long do your people typically live?" she asked.

"The average Solarus Zone citizen survives approximately three hundred and seventy Earth years," Solar answered. "Though warriors often face earlier termination due to combat risks."

"Three hundred and seventy years?" Dani's eyes widened. "And how old are you?"

"Seventy-eight Earth years."

She stared at him, clearly recalculating her

understanding of their relationship. "So you're basically in your twenties by our standards?"

"The comparison is approximate but acceptable," Solar confirmed.

Dani laughed softly, shaking her head. "Of course you are. I finally meet a guy who isn't emotionally stunted, and he turns out to be an alien barely out of adolescence with a three-century lifespan."

Solar wasn't entirely certain how to interpret this statement. "Does my relative youth concern you? I assure you, I am an honored warrior."

"No," she said, her smile softening as she reached for his hand. "It's just a lot to process. Everything is. Being in space. Leaving Earth. You."

Her touch created the now-familiar resonance in his energy field, a harmonization that felt both welcome and increasingly necessary. Solar found himself intensifying the connection, allowing more of his natural luminescence to flow through the contact point between them.

The ship lurched suddenly, the artificial gravity fluctuating. Solar instinctively steadied Dani, his arm circling her waist as the deck briefly tilted beneath them.

"That's the third time today," Dani observed once

the system stabilized. "Is this hunk of junk going to hold together?"

"Unlikely without significant intervention," Solar admitted. "I have identified seventeen critical systems requiring immediate attention. The propulsion stabilizers are particularly concerning."

"Show me," Dani said with surprising determination. "If we're stuck here, I might as well make myself useful."

Solar led her from the viewport room, navigating through the ship's confusing layout. Galaxy Brides' vessel was a patchwork of technologies joined with minimal regard for compatibility or safety protocols. Corridors ended abruptly in sealed bulkheads, panels labeled in a dozen different languages covered walls, and exposed wiring hung from ceilings like tropical vines.

"This is worse than I thought," Dani commented as they passed a section where the floor grating had been removed, revealing a tangle of pulsing tubes beneath. "How does this thing even fly?"

"That remains unclear," Solar replied honestly. "The propulsion system appears to incorporate at least three fundamentally incompatible power sources. I think it's gotten worse since we arrived on Earth. Alternatively, I suspect that Eclipse kept the ship in repair and did not inform us of the issue during the trip here. I am beginning to suspect I have not given Eclipse enough credit for his quiet temperament and peacekeeper role."

They reached a chamber that could be called the engine room, though it more closely resembled the aftermath of an explosion in a technology recycling facility. Equipment salvaged from various spacecraft had been bolted, welded, and in some cases simply tied together with metallic cording.

"This cannot be safe," Dani whispered, staring at a glowing cylindrical object suspended in what appeared to be a modified food preservation unit.

"It's not," Solar confirmed, moving to a control panel that displayed a constantly shifting array of warning indicators. "The primary power core is operating at one hundred and thirty-seven percent of its designed capacity. The thermal regulation system compensates by venting excess energy into the ship's water reclamation system."

"Which explains why the shower was steaming without being turned on," Dani realized. "So we're basically riding in a flying bomb?"

"The probability of catastrophic failure is significant but not immediate," Solar assured her, though his own assessment was less optimistic than his words suggested. He had been monitoring the deteriorating systems since their departure, and the degradation was accelerating.

Dani approached the makeshift control panel, studying the unfamiliar displays with obvious curiosity. "Can you keep teaching me how to help? I'm good with my hands, and I learn fast."

Solar considered her offer. The task of stabilizing the ship's systems was daunting, especially given the unplanned nature of the technology. Yet having observed Dani's precision with fire manipulation and her adaptability in crisis situations, he found himself nodding.

"Your assistance would be valuable," he acknowledged. "Though the work will be challenging and potentially dangerous."

"More dangerous than doing nothing?" Dani asked with a raised eyebrow.

Solar felt his energy pulse with something that might have been amusement. "Your point is valid."

Over the next several hours, Solar guided Dani through the basics of the ship's systems, teaching her to identify critical components and assess their functionality. Though the technology was alien to her, she demonstrated a remarkable ability to grasp underlying principles and apply them to unfamiliar contexts.

"So this converts the energy from the main drive into something the life support can use?" she asked, carefully reconnecting a series of color-coded conduits.

"Correct," Solar confirmed, impressed by her intuition. "The conversion matrix is essentially a universal adapter for incompatible power systems."

"Like trying to charge an iPhone with an Android cable," Dani muttered. "Except if you get it wrong, we all die."

Her ability to translate complex concepts into Earth analogies was both efficient and oddly endearing. Solar found himself increasingly drawn to the way her mind processed, practical yet creative, analytical yet intuitive.

As they worked, Solar became aware of subtle changes in his own behavior. He found himself creating reasons to demonstrate techniques that required physical proximity. His energy emissions shifted in response to her movements, almost as if seeking to align with her biorhythms.

These responses were not tactical. They served no mission objective. They were, he was beginning to realize, entirely personal.

"Hand me that coupling tool?" Dani requested, reaching out without looking up from the panel she was repairing.

Solar placed the instrument in her palm, deliberately allowing his fingers to brush against hers. The contact sent a pleasant resonance through his energy field that he made no effort to suppress.

Dani glanced up, a small smile playing at the corners of her mouth. "You did that on purpose."

"Yes," Solar admitted, seeing no tactical advantage in deception. "I find our energy exchange agreeable."

Her smile widened. "That's one way to put it." She returned to her work, but not before adding, "For the record, I find it agreeable too."

They continued their repairs, moving methodically through the ship's most critical systems. It reminded him of combat formations with his Elite Guard unit, but with a fundamental difference. His warriors followed his commands out of duty and training. Dani worked alongside him as an equal, her cooperation freely given, her insights offered without obligation.

The distinction was significant in ways Solar was still processing.

"I think we've done all we can with the stabilizers," Dani said finally, wiping sweat from her forehead with the back of her hand. "Unless you want to completely rebuild them, which might be easier than trying to fix this mess."

"The improvements are substantial," Solar assured her, reviewing the system diagnostics. "Catastrophic failure probability has decreased by forty-seven percent."

"Only a fifty-three percent chance of exploding? I'll take it," Dani quipped, though her expression remained serious. "What's next on the crisis list?"

The words felt like a sexual invitation, and he found himself starting to reach for her. But before Solar could respond, the ship lurched again, more violently this time. The lights flickered, plunging the engine room into momentary darkness before his natural radiance compensated by casting everything in a golden glow.

"That was not a stabilizer issue," Solar observed, moving quickly to check the control panel. "The gravitational compensators are failing."

"Is that bad?" Dani asked, bracing herself against a support beam.

"Not immediately life-threatening, but significant," Solar explained, his hands moving across the controls with practiced precision. "The artificial gravity field maintains our position within the vessel. Without it—"

The ship shuddered again, and suddenly they were weightless. Dani gasped as her feet left the floor, her body drifting upward. Solar, accustomed to zero-gravity combat training, immediately anchored himself to the control panel with one hand while reaching out to catch her with the other.

"I've got you," he assured her, pulling her close as they floated in the engine room's golden-lit space.

"This is different," Dani managed, her body pressed against his as she adjusted to the sensation of weightlessness. Her hair floated around her face, catching the light from his skin in a way that reminded him of flames.

Solar found his attention divided between the failing system and the feel of her supple warmth against his. Her energy signature pulsing in a pattern that increasingly felt like an extension of his own. The proximity was tactically unnecessary but personally desirable.

"I can restore gravity," he said, though he made no immediate move to do so. "It requires redirection of power from non-essential systems."

"Define non-essential," Dani replied, her fingers curling into the fabric of his shirt to stabilize herself.

The movement brought her face closer to his, close enough that he could feel her breath against his skin.

"Life support, propulsion, and defensive shields are essential," Solar listed automatically. "Entertainment systems, secondary lighting, and thermal comfort regulation are non-essential."

"So we'll be alive but cold and in the dark?" Dani summarized.

"Correct. Though my natural emissions can provide both light and heat."

Dani's eyes met his, something shifting in her expression. "Your natural emissions, huh? Those have been pretty useful so far."

The subtle change in her tone triggered an immediate response in Solar's energy field, causing his skin to brighten. He recognized the pattern from their previous encounter, the heightened biorhythms, the dilated pupils, the slight elevation in her body temperature. Signs of arousal.

"The repairs can wait," she said softly, her hand moving to touch his face. "We're already floating in zero gravity. Might as well take advantage of it, don't you think?"

Solar considered this suggestion. From a purely tactical perspective, system repairs should take priority. But he was discovering that not all decisions needed to be tactical.

"The gravity will eventually stabilize on its own," he reasoned, his hand sliding to her waist. "Approximately twenty-three minutes."

"Twenty-three minutes," Dani repeated, a smile spreading across her face. "That's not much time."

"I am capable of efficiency."

Her laugh was cut short as Solar closed the distance between them, his lips finding hers with precision that belied the unanchored environment. The kiss deepened immediately, both of them abandoning the tentative exploration of their first encounter. Now they knew each other's rhythms, understood the harmonics of their connection.

As they kissed, they rotated slowly in the zero-gravity environment, drifting away from the control panel toward the center of the engine room. Solar's natural light intensified, bathing them in golden radiance that pulsed in time with his quickening energy.

Dani's hands moved to his shirt, deftly unfastening it to reveal his luminescent skin beneath. "I missed this," she murmured against his mouth. "Seeing the real you."

Solar felt a surge of pleasure at her words. On Zorveya, his natural form was commonplace, unremarkable among his own kind. But Dani saw it as something extraordinary, something to be admired rather than concealed.

"The feeling is mutual," he replied, helping her remove her own shirt in the weightless environment. The garment drifted away, forgotten as he took in the sight of her partially unclothed form floating before him.

Their bodies came together again, skin against skin, his light flowing into her wherever they touched. In zero gravity, every movement created an equal and opposite reaction, sending them spinning slowly as they explored each other with increasing urgency.

Solar discovered that weightlessness offered new possibilities, new angles and positions that defied Earth's gravitational constraints. He used his warrior's training to control their rotation and to anchor them against the gentle drift that threatened to separate them.

"This is incredible," Dani gasped as Solar's mouth traced a path along her collarbone, down to the curve of her breast. Her head fell back, her hair floating around her like flame frozen in time.

"We have only begun," Solar assured her, his voice deepening as his control over his emissions slipped further. Light pulsed from his skin, growing brighter with his arousal, casting moving shadows across Dani's body that enhanced every curve, every contour.

They helped each other remove the remainder of their clothing, the garments drifting away. Fully naked now, they moved together in the weightless space, a dance more complex and intricate than any Solar had known. Without gravity's pull, every touch, every caress required deliberate intent, creating a heightened awareness of each point of contact.

Dani's hands explored his body with the same precision she'd shown in their repair work, finding the places where his energy concentrated, where his light flared brightest beneath her touch. Solar responded in kind, mapping the subtle electrical patterns of her nervous system, learning where pressure elicited the strongest response.

"You're getting brighter," she observed, her voice breathless as her fingers traced patterns across his chest.

"My control diminishes with arousal," Solar explained, watching golden motes of light break free from his skin to swirl around them both. "Is it uncomfortable for you?"

"Hell, no," Dani replied, pulling him closer. "It's beautiful. You're beautiful."

The simple statement affected Solar more deeply than he anticipated. Beauty was not a quality valued in the Solarus Elite Guard, where function and effectiveness were the only meaningful metrics. To be seen as beautiful, to be desired for more than strategic capability, created a resonance in his core energy that defied analysis.

Their bodies aligned perfectly as they came together. Her legs wrapped around his waist, and he knew what she wanted him to do. His essence molded to fit inside her, stretching her as he pulsed. Solar guided them with subtle adjustments that kept them centered in the engine room's space as Dani pushed her hips to his.

Dani gasped, her fingers digging into his shoulders as they moved together. Without gravity to work against, each thrust created momentum that required careful control, a rhythm that built gradually as they learned to navigate this new environment.

Solar felt his energy expanding beyond the boundaries of his physical form, golden light encompassing them both in a private universe of shared sensation. Where their bodies joined, the transfer of energy intensified, creating feedback loops of pleasure that cycled between them and built with each movement.

"Solar," Dani whispered, her eyes wide as she watched light flow across her skin like fire where they touched. "What's happening?"

"Energy alignment," he managed, his voice strained as he fought to maintain some measure of control. "Our signatures are harmonizing."

The harmonization was deeper than anything Solar had experienced before, a synchronization of energy that surpassed physical coupling. As they moved together, floating in the center of the engine room, the boundaries between them seemed to blur. His light flowed into her, and her electrical patterns influenced his emissions.

The ship around them faded until only Dani existed. He focused on the sound of her breathing, the heat of her skin, the way her energy signature pulsed in time with his own. Their movements accelerated, finding a rhythm that defied the weightless environment, each thrust perfectly counterbalanced to maintain their position.

Solar felt the approaching climax, the point beyond which his control would shatter completely. His light intensified further, a radiance that filled the engine room so that the walls seemed to be replaced by a universe of pure energy.

"I can't—" Dani gasped, her body arching against his, her eyes wide with building pleasure.

"Don't fight it," Solar urged, his hands guiding her movements. "Let our energies align."

The alignment, when it came, was simultaneous and overwhelming. Solar felt his emissions surge beyond any previous limits as Dani cried out, her body convulsing against his. For one transcendent moment, he couldn't distinguish where his energy field ended and hers began. They were a single system, a perfect harmonic resonance cascading through shared consciousness.

The surge was so powerful that it traveled through the ship's systems, momentarily stabilizing the failing gravitational compensators. Gravity suddenly returned, dropping them to the floor. Solar instinctively positioned himself to absorb the impact. He landed on his feet with a light thud on the deck plating, cradling her in his arms, still joined, still engulfed in his light.

For several moments, they remained perfectly still, her breathing gradually slowing. The brighter light slowly receded to a gentle glow.

"That," Dani finally said, her voice hushed with

awe, "was definitely not in any Earth physics textbook."

Solar felt something unfamiliar move through his energy field. The sensation manifested physically as a slight upward curve of his lips. "Nor in Zorveyan combat manuals."

Dani laughed, the sound vibrating pleasantly through their still-joined bodies. "I think you just fixed the gravity with an orgasm."

"A temporary solution," Solar replied, his hand moving to trace the curve of her face. "But an effective one. My energy does feel stronger than before, like I stood in sunlight for an hour."

"We should probably test it again," Dani suggested, her eyes meeting his with a warmth that created ripples through his energy field. "You know, for scientific thoroughness."

Solar considered this proposal, analyzing their position, the ship's status, and the remaining repairs. All logical considerations pointed to resuming work immediately.

"The scientific method does require multiple trials to establish validity," he agreed instead, his light brightening as she smiled.

Before she could answer, the ship's communication system activated with a harsh static burst.

"Solar! Dani!" Gary's voice echoed through the engine room. "Emergency transmission incoming from the surface. Report to the command center immediately."

They exchanged glances, the moment of connection shifting as duty reasserted itself.

"To be continued," Dani promised, pressing a quick kiss to his lips before reaching for her clothing that had been sprinkled around the room when the gravity came back on.

Solar nodded, already calculating the most efficient path to the command center while simultaneously processing what had just occurred between them.

Dani was, he had begun to understand, something worth fighting for... perhaps even more so than his duty to Zorveya.

15

IN THE COMMAND CENTER, BOB WAS frantically adjusting controls. His oversized head bobbed with stress. Gary paced behind him, wringing his hands.

"What is the nature of the emergency?" Solar demanded.

"We established a transmission link from the surface," Gary explained, gesturing to a display showing a fragmented signal pattern. "Encrypted using Galaxy Brides protocols, but the signal is weak."

"Origin point?" Solar moved to the console, analyzing the data with practiced efficiency.

"Here. We originated it," Bob said.

"I mean on Earth. Who are you talking to?" Solar said.

"It is connected to the southwestern region of the designated North American continent," Bob replied, his usual incompetence momentarily suppressed by the situation's gravity. "But precise coordinates are unclear due to signal degradation."

"How can they be unclear? You did it." Solar accessed the communications array, making rapid adjustments to boost reception. The fragmented pattern gradually stabilized, resolving into a recognizable encryption sequence.

"You look different somehow," Gary said, eyeing him and then Dani. A strange look crossed his face, and Solar swore the alien was smiling.

"It's Lunar," Solar announced, ignoring Gary. "They think Milano has captured Eclipse."

Dani moved to his side, her expression grim. "When?"

"During Rowan and my escape from the caves. He hasn't resurfaced." Solar translated the message that continued to form on the display. "They're hiding in a cabin."

"Fuck," Dani whispered. "Do they know where they took him?"

Solar continued to decipher the message as it

scrolled across the screen. "They don't know. They want us to look for his energy signatures from our location to see if we can track him."

Dani's hand found Solar's arm. "There must be something we can do."

Solar considered their options. "Galaxy Brides' alternative extraction protocol uses energy signature recognition. Each of us carries a unique pattern that their systems can lock onto. If Eclipse's signature can be enhanced, we may be able to help locate him."

"That's exactly what I was going to suggest," Bob inserted.

Dani frowned at the alien. "Well, what are we waiting for? Let's do it."

"There is risk," Solar cautioned. "Amplifying Eclipse's energy signature would also make our position more detectable to Milano's tracking systems."

"But we'd be helping Eclipse," Dani countered, her eyes intent on his. "We can't just leave him to Milano's scientists. What if it were you? He wouldn't leave you behind."

Solar understood her concern. Eclipse was more than a mission comrade. He was a fellow Zorveyan, one who had shown unexpected tactical flexibility and personal courage. The Elite Guard code emphasized victory above all, but it also acknowledged the strategic value of preserving skilled operatives.

Something deeper stirred within Solar. A sense of obligation. Of connection. Eclipse had remained behind to allow their escape. Honor demanded reciprocation.

"I will attempt the amplification," Solar decided. "Bob, prepare the sensor array for reconfiguration. Gary, monitor Earth's orbital detection systems for any sign of Milano activity."

"Give Lunar a new extraction timeline before you disconnect," Bob ordered Gary. "Let him know we'll be there in fourteen Earth days. Tell him to remain where he is. That will give us time to liaise with Harris on Earth."

For once, both aliens worked without unnecessary commentary. Solar moved to the main sensor control panel, his light brightening as he channeled energy directly into the ship's systems.

The process was delicate. Solar's natural energy had to be carefully modulated to avoid overwhelming the ship's already unstable systems.

"Is it working?" Dani asked.

"The signal is strengthening," Solar confirmed, monitoring the energy patterns displayed on the screen.

As the amplification continued, a map of Earth's surface terrain appeared on the main display, gradually focusing on a specific region. A pulsing point of light emerged, growing stronger as Solar channeled more energy into the system.

"There," he indicated the light. "Eclipse's energy signature. He is being held in a subterranean facility approximately forty kilometers from their current position."

"Can we send this information to Lunar?" Dani asked.

"Starting transmission," Solar confirmed, automatically relaying the coordinates through the encrypted channel.

A warning indicator flashed on a secondary display.

"Stop!" Bob lurched forward, his expression alarmed. "Energy detection alert. Something on the surface is scanning us."

Solar immediately reduced his emissions.

"What's happening?" Dani asked, concern evident in her voice.

"Milano has detected our energy signature," Bob continued. "They are attempting to lock onto our position. You can't contact Lunar again. You'll reveal his position."

"Do they know we're here?" Dani insisted. "And that we're helping them?"

"Yes," Solar acknowledged.

"We need to warn them," Dani insisted.

"Not yet. Eclipse is in immediate danger. Lunar and the others are safe so long as we don't expose them." Solar assured her.

"If Milano has detected us, our extraction timeline is compromised," Gary interjected, his usual bravado absent.

"They can't reach us in space right now," Solar denied. "Earth's launch capabilities are limited, and Milano would face significant obstacles in deploying any vessel capable of orbital interception without detection by Earth authorities."

"Agreed," Gary said, like he had the same idea.

Solar sighed. "We must prepare for immediate relocation. Bob, calculate alternative orbital positions that would minimize detection while monitoring when it is safe to communicate with the surface."

Bob frantically worked the navigation controls.

"They're getting better at tracking us," Dani observed, watching the warning indicators multiply across the displays.

"Their technology is adapting," Solar confirmed.

She moved closer to him and clutched his arm. "We have to help them."

"If there is a way, I will find it," he whispered, letting threads of his energy weave over her hands in what he hoped was comfort. "I promise."

THE RESCUE MISSION WAS A MESS. Solar stood in the command center staring at the controls for so long that they began to blur in his vision. Dani tried to stand with him, but humans needed sleep, and he'd insisted she rest.

In the end, all he could do was stretch the signal Eclipse tried to send to Rowan on the surface to make sure it reached her. The woman carried Eclipse's energy stone. It was not a power source Milano appeared to be tracking. From there, he had to have faith Rowan would know what to do.

He did not like acting on faith.

Dani entered holding a nutrient pouch. She handed it to him. "You need to eat."

He set the pouch aside, not consuming it. "Rowan is attempting infiltration of the Milano facility."

"She's going in alone?" Dani asked in concern.

"Eclipse is showing her the way," Solar explained.

Dani shook her head, admiration clear in her expression. "That woman has guts."

"Indeed," Solar agreed, finding himself equally impressed by the Earth female's courage. "Her tactical initiative is commendable."

For the next several hours, all they could do was watch and hope. Solar did not like the helpless feeling it gave him. Dani stared at the console, as if it might give her the answers she waited for, but only time could do that.

"Rowan has reached Eclipse," Solar watched Eclipse's energy signature dispersing over the desert. Relief filled him. "They're out of the facility, but Milano is giving chase."

"Fuck waiting fourteen days," Dani said, sighing heavily as if coming to a decision. "Tell Bob and Gary we're going back now. The extraction happens tonight. No more desert chases."

16

Dani pressed her face against the observation port, watching the blue-white marble of Earth spin slowly below. Somewhere down there, their friends were running for their lives. And all she could do was watch.

"Anything?" Solar asked from his position at the communications console.

"Nothing new," she replied, fighting the urge to punch the reinforced glass. "Just Milano forces converging on the extraction coordinates."

The command center of Galaxy Brides' ship felt more claustrophobic than ever. Bob and Gary fluttered around various controls, their oversized heads bobbing with anxiety as they monitored the situation on the surface.

"Extraction window opens in twelve minutes," Gary announced for the third time. "Harris is in position with the others."

"We should be down there," Dani muttered, her fingers clenching and unclenching. "Not floating up here like useless—"

An alarm shrieked through the ship. Red lights began flashing across multiple consoles.

"What now?" Dani demanded, spinning toward the controls.

Bob's yellow skin had gone pale. "The extraction field... It's destabilizing."

Solar moved immediately to the sensor array, his golden light intensifying as he analyzed the data streaming across the displays. "The energy matrix is unbalanced. It requires three distinct signatures to form properly. Didn't you tell Harris to reset it?"

"So?" Dani asked, not understanding.

"Solar's light energy is here," Bob explained frantically. "Eclipse's twilight energy is severely depleted from his captivity. The field cannot stabilize without proper triangulation."

"Can't you fix it from here?" Dani pressed.

Gary shook his head so vigorously it looked like it might detach. "Field parameters locked at surface level. Need physical presence to adjust."

Dani watched Solar's expression harden as he processed the implications. The extraction field would collapse without balance. And if it collapsed...

"The dimensional bridge is going to implode," Solar stated. "It will destroy any chance they have of coming home, and potentially damage our vessel if we're still connected to the energy stream."

"Sever the connection. We can't let them attempt it," Dani said immediately. "Let's fly down and get them."

"Cannot," Bob wailed. "Extraction protocols engage automatic link with mothership. Safety feature!"

"Safety feature my ass," Dani growled. "So we're saying Eclipse can't make the extraction because he's too weak, but if he doesn't, we all die? And if Solar can't somehow go down there and travel back up with them, we all die?"

"Not necessarily," Solar interrupted, his calm flowing over her. She could practically see his mind working through scenarios. "Lunar's shadow energy could substitute. His signature is strong enough to balance the field. He could make the trip alone."

Dani felt her heart sink. "What about Poppy?"

Through the viewport, she could see the faint glow beginning to form at the extraction coordinates.

The field attempted to establish itself despite the imbalance.

"Incoming transmission," Gary announced, his fingers dancing over controls.

Harris' panicked voice filled the command center. "Problem. Big problem. Extraction field unstable. Energy matrix destabilizing!"

"Can we talk to them directly?" she asked.

"Negative," Bob replied. "Energy interference from the unstable field. Harris is barely getting through."

Solar leaned forward, his golden light pulsing with intensity. "Harris, this is Solar. Tell Lunar he must take Eclipse's position in the extraction field. I can try to supplement his energy from here. His shadow energy can stabilize the matrix."

There was static, then Harris' voice again. "Eclipse too... Lunar saying..." More static. "...must go up. Must warn about Milano."

Dani felt tears prick her eyes.

"Five minutes to extraction," Gary whispered, his usual cheer absent.

Through the sensors, they could see Milano forces closing in on the extraction site. Helicopters swept searchlights across the desert. Ground vehicles kicked up dust clouds as they raced toward the coordinates.

"They're not going to make it," Dani whispered.

Solar's hand found her shoulder, his warmth steady and reassuring. "Lunar is resourceful. He will ensure the extraction succeeds."

"But at what cost?" Dani turned to face him. "He loves Poppy. You've seen them together. And now he has to leave her behind?"

"Sometimes duty requires sacrifice," Solar said quietly, though she could hear the conflict in his voice.

Dani felt a cold chill at the thought. What would Solar have to sacrifice? What would she?

The extraction field on the surface began to pulse more rapidly, its glow visible even from orbit as the energy built to critical levels.

"Field stabilizing," Bob announced suddenly. "Shadow signature detected. Lunar is in position."

Dani pressed against the viewport again, as if she could somehow see the individual figures from orbit. All she could make out was the growing glow of the extraction field and the converging lights of Milano vehicles.

"Milano forces have reached the perimeter," Gary reported. "Weapons discharge detected."

"Eclipse," Solar said suddenly, his attention focused on a separate display showing energy signatures. "He's shielding the others. Using his remaining twilight energy to protect Rowan and Poppy."

"Can he hold it?" Dani asked.

Solar's expression was grim. "Not for long. Not in his depleted state."

The extraction field flared a brilliant white, temporarily overloading their sensors. When the displays cleared, one signature was rising rapidly from the surface.

"Extraction successful," Bob announced. "Lunar is on the dimensional bridge and clear of the atmosphere."

"What about Eclipse and the others?" Dani demanded.

Solar adjusted the sensors, scanning for the familiar energy patterns. "Eclipse created a diversion during the extraction flash. They're moving away from Milano forces."

"But they're still being pursued," Dani observed, watching the Milano signatures reorganizing and giving chase.

"Confirm Harris' pod trajectory," Solar ordered.

Gary checked his instruments. "On course. ETA seven minutes."

Seven minutes. Then Lunar would be here, alone, having left behind the woman who'd somehow cracked through his cold exterior. Dani thought about how that would feel, being ripped away from someone you'd just found, someone who understood you in ways no one else could.

Her hand found Solar's, their fingers intertwining. She couldn't imagine being separated from him now. The thought of it created a physical ache in her chest.

"Eclipse is leading them into the canyon systems," Solar reported, still monitoring the surface. "Using the terrain to break pursuit. Clever tactics for a diplomat."

"Will they escape?" Dani asked.

"Unknown. Milano's technology is sophisticated. But Eclipse knows the desert now. And he's protecting the others." A note of respect entered Solar's voice. "He fights well for one trained in peace."

The docking alert sounded. Through the forward viewport, they could see the small craft wobbling slightly as it aligned with their docking port next to a dark shadow streaking toward the ship.

"That's not a smooth approach," Dani observed.

"Harris' piloting skills are..." Solar paused, searching for a diplomatic word.

"Shit," Dani supplied. "His piloting skills are shit."

"Accurate," Solar agreed.

The small pod connected with a jarring clang that reverberated through the ship. The docking clamps engaged with a grinding sound, suggesting that something wasn't quite aligned properly.

"Successful dock," Gary announced, apparently unconcerned by the mechanical protests. "Our passengers are aboard!"

Dani was already moving toward the airlock, Solar close behind. She needed to see Lunar to understand what had happened and to know if their friends were truly safe.

The airlock opened, and Harris stumbled out. His skin suit was torn in several places, and he looked even more disheveled than usual.

"Pudding!" he announced.

"Pudding indeed," Bob answered. "Come on, let's fix your translator."

Harris began chattering in a strange language, and Bob answered in kind.

Behind him, Lunar flowed into the ship's port like a liquid shadow. His form was more condensed than usual, pulled tight with control. Even in his alien shape, Dani could read the tension, the carefully suppressed emotion.

"Lunar," she said softly. "I'm so sorry."

The shadow being's form rippled slightly. "The extraction was successful. That is what matters."

"Bullshit," Dani muttered.

The others looked at her in surprise.

"You left her behind," she said. "You left Poppy behind because the field needed your energy. I don't count that as a successful anything."

"The mission required—"

"Fuck the mission," Dani interrupted. "You love her."

Lunar went absolutely still. For a moment, Dani thought she'd overstepped, pushed too hard. Then his form shifted, becoming more solid. His eyes turned away, and he didn't answer.

Solar stepped forward. "Eclipse and the others? What is their status?"

"Eclipse wants to remain, not that he had a choice. The extraction would have killed him," Lunar reported, his voice keeping its usual controlled tone. "His twilight energy was too depleted for the journey, and someone needed to protect Rowan and Poppy from Milano."

"He can do that? He can stay?" Dani asked, hopeful that Solar might want to do the same.

"The council will consider him in dereliction of duty," Lunar said, "unless we can convince them it was for the best he stayed behind."

Solar wouldn't meet her gaze, and she could only stare at him.

"He could not return, so you came back to report about Milano," Solar concluded.

"The threat assessment is critical," Lunar said. "The weapons they've developed, their knowledge of our physiology, their intention to expand beyond Earth... The council must be warned."

"And then what?" Dani asked. "After you make your report?"

Lunar's form shifted again, something almost like hope flickering through the shadows. "Then I will request authorization to return. To establish formal diplomatic relations. To assess the continuing threat."

"To see Poppy again," Dani said softly.

"Yes," Lunar admitted. "To see Poppy again, but I will not tell the council that."

Bob bustled into the airlock area. "Beautiful reunion, very touching, but we have a problem. Milano detected our orbital position during the extraction. They're mobilizing resources."

"They can't reach us here," Solar stated.

"No, but they can make planet-side operations very difficult," Bob replied. "Every potential landing site, they'll be watching."

"Then we avoid Earth for now," Gary said, appearing behind Bob. "Continue to Zorveya as planned. Make an official report to the corporation. Request a formal mission with proper resources and authority. I hear there is a nice planet in the X quadrant with men who turn into strange creatures. We can try that location."

"We can't tell the corporation what happened," Bob denied before chattering away in his alien language.

"Dani belongs on Earth. You can't force her to leave her planet," Solar said.

Dani felt something settle in her chest. It was the decision she'd been unconsciously making since they'd left Earth's surface. "No."

Everyone turned to look at her.

"No?" Solar asked, his golden light pulsing with curiosity.

"We're not running away to Zorveya never to return while our friends are being hunted," Dani said firmly. "Eclipse, Rowan, and Poppy cannot be sacrificed because it's *easier* than going back and dealing with the mess."

"What do you propose?" Lunar asked, his shadow form leaning forward with interest.

Dani looked at Solar, seeing her own determination reflected in his golden eyes. "We go to Zorveya. All of us. The two of you make your report to the council. Tell them everything about Milano, about Earth's potential as an ally, about the connections we've formed. Then we come back with a real ship, real resources, and we finish what we started."

"The council may not approve," Solar warned. "They sent us here to fail, remember?"

"Then we make them approve," Dani said. "You're a warrior. Lunar's an intelligence specialist. I'm..." she paused, then smiled. "I'm a fire dancer who's apparently compatible with alien energy signatures. Between us, we can make them listen."

"And if they refuse?" Lunar asked.

Dani's smile widened. "Then we steal a ship and come back anyway."

Solar's golden light flared brighter. "That would be a significant violation of Zorveyan law."

"Good thing I'm not Zorveyan," Dani replied. She turned to Lunar. "Poppy's waiting for you. Eclipse and Rowan are counting on us. Are we really going to abandon them?"

Lunar's shadow form straightened, decision crystallizing in his posture. "No. We are not."

"This is highly irregular," Bob protested. "Galaxy Brides cannot support unsanctioned—"

"Galaxy Brides got us into this mess," Dani cut him off. "Your matchmaking service sent three aliens to Earth with failing equipment and no support. You're lucky we're not filing a complaint with whatever passes for human-alien resource departments in the galaxy."

Gary made a sound that might have been a laugh. "She has a point, Bob. We wouldn't want complaints filed."

Bob threw up his hands. "Fine. But Galaxy Brides takes no responsibility for any subsequent actions."

"Understood," Solar said. Then, to Dani, "You're certain about this? Zorveya is unlike Earth. My people value strength and light above all else. You may find it—"

"Solar," Dani interrupted, taking his hands. "Your planet is basically one giant sunbath, right? Eternal daylight, fire, and energy everywhere?"

"Essentially, yes."

"That's literally my dream vacation," she said. "Plus, I get to see where you grew up, meet your people, and help convince them that Earth is worth protecting. How is this even a question?"

Solar's expression softened in that way she'd learned meant he was processing emotions he didn't quite have words for. "You continue to surprise me."

"Good," Dani said. "I'd hate to be predictable."

She felt the ship's engines rumble to life as Bob and Gary prepared for the journey to Zorveya. Twenty-seven days through space to an alien world where she'd have to help convince an entire civilization that Earth—*messy, chaotic, beautiful Earth*—was worth saving.

Twenty-seven days to figure out how to make the council see what she knew. Love transcended alien species. Connection could cross galaxies. And sometimes, the mission parameters needed to change.

"So," Dani said, looking between Solar and Lunar. "Who's going to teach me basic Zorveyan? I'm guessing, *'please don't incinerate the Earth girl,'* might be a useful phrase."

Despite everything, Solar's golden light pulsed with amusement.

"I will prepare the universal translator for implantation," Bob stated.

"First lesson," he said. "On Zorveya, fire does not dance. It works."

"Well," Dani replied, "then I guess I'll be teaching them a few things too."

As the ship turned away from Earth, beginning its long journey to an alien sun, Dani allowed herself one last look at her home planet. Somewhere down there, Eclipse and Rowan were building a life together while staying one step ahead of Milano. Poppy was waiting, probably already working on a way to communicate across the stars.

At least, that's what she hoped.

They'd be back. All of them. Together.

"You are an amazing creature," Solar whispered. "I will forever only resonate with you."

"I love you, too," Dani answered.

The mission had changed, evolved into something none of them had expected. But maybe that was the point. Maybe the real success wasn't in following parameters but in discovering what happened when those parameters shattered.

Twenty-seven days to Zorveya. Then, one way or another, they were coming home.

"Hey, Solar?" she said as Earth shrank in the viewport.

"Yes?"

"Is it really made of fire? Your zone? Because I had this whole mental image..."

Solar's patient explanation of solar radiation versus actual combustion filled the command center as they sailed into the black, three unlikely allies bound by a common purpose.

Bring their people home. Protect Earth. And prove that love—*weird, impossible, interspecies love*—could conquer even the vast distances between stars.

Game on, Milano. Game fucking on.

The End

Galaxy Alien Mail Order Brides Series

Spark

Flame

Blaze

Ice

Frost

Snow

Eclipse Bound

Solar Bound

Lunar Bound

Lunar Bound

Sci-fi Paranormal Romantic Comedy

He hunts in shadows. She shines a light he can't resist.

When three aliens crash into Duskrock, Arizona, empath and wildlife rehabilitator Poppy Jensen senses what no one else can—Lunar, a shadow-born operative from Zorveya's night side, made to move unseen. He expects fear. She offers a hand. One touch sparks more than either imagined, and suddenly secrecy is impossible.

Lunar never wanted to join Galaxy Alien Mail Order Brides on this ill-conceived mission, but his leaders gave him no choice. Now stranded on a strange planet and hunted by a ruthless black-ops outfit, survival depends on a woman who should never have been able to see him at all.

On the run through desert nights and hidden caves, forced proximity fans their connection into something undeniable. Lunar speaks in actions, and Poppy understands every one. With hunters closing in and extraction running out of time, he must decide if protecting his mission is worth losing the one woman who makes the darkness feel like home.

--

LUNAR BOUND is a steamy sci-fi paranormal romantic comedy with a grumpy alien and a sunshine empath, shadow-walking danger, hunted lovers on the run, sizzling open-door heat, and a guaranteed HEA with no cliffhanger.

Book three of the Bound Trilogy installment from the Galaxy Alien Mail Order Brides series.

Updated Reading List and Links here: MichellePillow.com

MICHELLE M. PILLOW NOVELS

Free Reading Guides

Download free reading guides at
MichellePillow.com.

ABOUT THE AUTHOR

New York Times & *USA TODAY* Bestselling Author

Michelle loves to travel and try new things, whether it's a paranormal investigation of an old Vaudeville Theatre or climbing Mayan temples in Belize. She believes life is an adventure fueled by copious amounts of coffee.

Newly relocated to the American South, Michelle is involved in various film and documentary projects with her talented director husband. She is mom to a fantastic artist. And she's managed by a dog and cat who make sure she's meeting her deadlines.

For the most part she can be found wearing pajama pants and working in her office. There may or may not be dancing. It's all part of the creative process.

Come say hello! Michelle loves talking with readers on social media!

www.MichellePillow.com

facebook.com/AuthorMichellePillow

x.com/michellepillow

instagram.com/michellempillow

bookbub.com/authors/michelle-m-pillow

goodreads.com/Michelle_Pillow

amazon.com/author/michellepillow

youtube.com/michellepillow

pinterest.com/michellepillow

PLEASE LEAVE A REVIEW

THANK YOU FOR READING!

Please take a moment to share your thoughts by reviewing this book.

Be sure to check out Michelle's other titles at www.MichellePillow.com

Imprint

The Raven Books LLC
1723 University Ave Suite B #247
Oxford MS 38655
United States

Telephone Number: 1 (662) 484-4174
Email: theravenbooks@gmail.com
CEO: Michelle M. Pillow
Website: michellepillow.com

Please Leave a Review

Please take a moment to share your thoughts by reviewing this book.

Be sure to check out Michelle's other titles at www.MichellePillow.com

THANK YOU FOR READING!

Imprint

The Raven Books LLC
1723 University Ave Suite B #247
Oxford MS 38655
United States

Telephone Number: 1 (662) 484-4174
Email: theravenbooks@gmail.com
CEO: Michelle M. Pillow
Website: michellepillow.com